Eden kicked off the heels and scooted to the end of the bed. Her dress rode up her thighs in the process, and she caught Jack eyeing her legs.

"Turn away," she said. "Or haven't you the decency to give a girl a little privacy?"

"You can have all the privacy you want, Eden. I'm leaving."

"I don't want you to leave, Jack," she blurted out.

He stopped but didn't turn to look at her. "What do you want?" he asked. "I can't figure you out."

"I want you to stay and talk with me. I want to get to know you."

He turned his head slightly and eyed her again. He took a deep breath and released it.

"I can't stay," he muttered, facing the door again. "If I do, I won't be able to control myself. I've only had one thing on my mind since I saw you in that damned sexy dress. If you ask me to stay, I'm going to do something I may regret in the morning."

"Close the door, Jack. Regrets are only for those who live in the past. In Peru, we live for the day."

. . . . Jack gave a silent nod, then closed and locked the door.

Eden's Garden

ELIZABETH ROSE

Tango 2 is an imprint of
Genesis Press, Inc.
315 Third Avenue North
Columbus, Mississippi 39701

Eden's Garden

ISBN 1-58571-018-0

Manufactured in the United States of America

FIRST EDITION

To my husband, Michael, for believing in me and my dream, and helping me succeed.

To my sons, Jeffrey and Ryan, for being patient and understanding. Your love has given me the courage to see this through.

To my parents; and siblings Sue, Julie and Mike for sharing in my joy and always being there for me.

To the Windy City Romance writers for walking the road with me, especially Elysa Hendricks and Dyanne Davis for reading and critiquing anything I throw at them.

To Wednesday night writer's workshop: Kay, David, Rich, Mary, Kurt and Joe. Your sincerity and dedication is uplifting. I'll make romance readers out of you yet!

To my cover model Myra Glosny. Thanks for being Eden for a day. You were perfect!

To the employees at Downers Grove Post Office. Your smiling faces throughout my years of trying have helped me to continue.

To the staff at Genesis Press, especially Ann Marie South-Dollar, and my editor Karla Hocker. You have helped me more than you'll ever know.

And to my readers. Thank you for giving me a chance. I hope my writing will win a place in your hearts.

Eden's Garden

Chapter I

The air hung heavy in the cemetery as Eden watched her father's casket being lowered slowly into the ground. She knew she should cry and spill the pent up emotions that trapped her soul within her Incan shell, but she was raised by her mother to be stronger than that. Her culture accepted death as well as life. Her people very rarely cried at all.

Chicago's spring and scent of rain that clung to the city air only made her long for the mountains of Cuzco, Peru. The Andes were higher than heaven itself. A place where she felt close to God. This place, the home of her late father, Professor Jonathan Starke, was constructed of manmade stone. Concrete. A mere oven of the devil as she saw it in her own mind.

She toyed with the heart-shaped locket that hung from a yarn around her neck. It was her last remembrance of her father, the treasured icon of a man she loved yet barely knew. Thoughts of two days earlier drifted through her mind. The day she first set foot in the United States per her dying father's request.

"Eden . . . sweetheart . . . daughter."

His words in her own Quechua language had engraved their spot upon her heart. A mere few words thrown out carelessly into the universe as they rolled easily from his tongue, but it meant the world and more to her to hear the small endearment. He had called for her to be at his death bed . . . and he'd sent for her instead of her mother.

"Papa . . . don't die," she said in her native tongue. She took his large hand in hers and rubbed it softly against her cheek. He was so unlike the hardened professor who had come from the States year after year to study the Incan ruins of Machu Picchu, hoping to find some uncovered truth or hidden treasure of the ancient culture that was destroyed so many years ago.

"I wanted to marry your mother . . . really," he whispered through his ragged breathing. "I'm sorry." He struggled for breath. "I wish I could have been the father you needed."

Eden, in all her twenty years, had never once asked her father to stay when he'd made his yearly trip to Machu Picchu, stopping at her native rural village just outside of Cuzco during his expedition. She had never asked him, but in her heart she always wanted to beg him to stay. Yet he'd taken her with him on trips to Lima during his visits, and even to climb the peak of Huayna Picchu—the peak so high it touched the heavens itself. And now she was at his side again—only this time it would be the last.

"Take this, Eden. It's my gift to you." His trembling hand opened, and he held out a heart-shaped locket. He pressed it into her hand carefully as if it was the most precious thing he owned.

She didn't even look at the locket, just kept her eyes focused on her father's face. She wanted to have one last vision that would last her a life time. She only saw him once a year, and now she'd never see him again. She blinked her dry eyes, not allowing herself to feel the emotions that were building within her chest. They weren't important. It didn't matter. She was the farmer daughter of a mountain woman and nothing more. Her silent dreams of someday really knowing and understanding her father would die along with the man on the bed.

He opened his eyes and motioned with his head for her to open the nightstand drawer. His apartment was small, the pieces of furniture few and old. Why he lived this way instead of the way a man of his importance should, she didn't understand. And why he chose to die at home with only her and a nurse nearby was another thing she couldn't comprehend.

She reluctantly let go of him with one hand and slid open the drawer. In it sat a Bible and a small burlap bag tied with a coarse rope.

"Take them," he whispered. "They are my remembrances of you."

She didn't understand at all, and couldn't think at the moment how to ask him what he meant. He was slipping back into the English language. And though he'd taught her his language, and she knew it well, she suddenly felt she couldn't remember a word of it.

"Papa," she whispered, but was too choked up to say more.

"Take the bag . . . give it to Jack. . . to help pay my debt."

Again, she didn't know what he meant. He had told her of his friend Jack Talon and that she should go to him when he passed on to the afterlife. He said this man would help her get home.

"I love you, Eden," were his last words before he closed his eyes never to open them again. She didn't return the words of love though she wanted to. Instead she let his hand slip from her grip as she allowed the nurse to pull her away.

The room was suddenly filled with people dressed in white. The old lady from the next apartment was there also and put her arm around Eden's shoulder.

"Come . . . my home," was all Eden heard her say. She turned back to her father lying on the bed and took one last glimpse of his face before the people in white covered it up with a sheet. She gripped the locket tightly in her hand and gingerly plucked the Bible and burlap bag from the drawer before letting the old lady escort her away from the father she would never get to know.

Jack Talon stopped his Mercedes convertible just up the road from where they were lowering Professor Jonathan Starke into the ground. This was one funeral he wasn't going to miss. He pushed open the door and stretched out his long legs as he made his way quickly toward the small group of people weeping for the dead man. Jack held no remorse for the way he felt. The man had turned into a disgrace ever since the University let him go last year. He then disappeared from society. Lucky for Jack his private investigator had found out about the professor's death.

For nearly a year Jack had waited for this day. Professor Jonathan Starke was nothing more than a fake. He'd told Jack he would make him rich and famous when he brought back the Incan secrets and hidden treasures to the Field Museum. Jack had lent him the money because he believed in the man. And he wanted to help if he could, but now he wished he hadn't. There was no fortune, no fame. And now that there was no professor, Jack's money was gone as well. It was his father's money he'd used, thinking he could make The Golden Talon restaurant more than it already was. The restaurant, his father told him, would be his if he could run it smoothly and show him he could handle his business dealings wisely.

The restaurant had been struggling for the last six months, but now all that would change. Jack had finally tracked down the man who disappeared with his money, and one way or another he was going to get it back. He had told Elliot Kempler, his friend and P.I., to meet him here at the cemetery. The professor must have been investing the money in some huge dealings and collecting the profits, just not wanting to share them with him. And Jack swore he'd get every penny back, plus interest for having to wait.

"Elliot." Jack extended a hand to his private investigator.

"Jack." Elliot pumped his hand quickly, keeping his voice low as he spoke. "Almost thought you weren't going to show."

"Ha! And miss this? Not on your life." Jack didn't bother to scan the grounds or even give the casket a second glance as it disappeared into the earth. He didn't care anymore. He had once felt compassion and friendship for the professor but now he despised the man for what he'd done to him.

"So how much is he worth?" he asked Elliot. "How much are we going to be able to get?"

"Nothing, Jack."

"What?" he said a bit louder than he should have. A ragged-looking, overweight woman turned to look at Jack. He smiled politely and lowering his voice turned back to Elliot. "What do you mean, nothing? That man owes me a lot of money."

"It was an investment, Jack."

"Like hell it was. Investments give you something in return. I got nothing."

Jack blew air from his mouth thinking of how disappointed his father would be once he returned from Europe. And he'd be back this autumn. Jack still had hopes to get his father's restaurant back in shape. If he could just recover his money, it might not be all that bad.

"Didn't you find any information about him hiding ancient trinkets or something on the side?" Jack asked.

He knew by the somber look on Elliot's face that the news wasn't going to be good.

"Let's go talk about this over lunch, Jack."

"I'm not hungry! Now tell me what's up before I blow my cool."

"You're not going to like this."

"I don't like one stinking thing about this whole damned deal, Elliot. Now hurry up and give it to me straight. I've got to get back to the restaurant to put in an order by noon."

"You'd better hold off on that order," said Elliot. "You may not be able to pay for it."

"What is that supposed to mean?" Jack's voice was getting louder again, and as the priest conducted the prayer service, the bystanders threw Jack angered looks though their lips spoke the words of God.

"It means Professor Starke was flat broke. He'd been gambling it away on the riverboat. Seems he drank a lot of it away also."

Jack felt his blood boiling and clenched his fists. "This can't be happening, Elliot. It's going to ruin me."

This day was going from bad to worse. The refrigeration units in the restaurant were on the fritz, and he just found out his taxes were being raised. And then his father called from Greece this morning and told him he'd be back in about four or five months to see how Jack was running the business. Jack needed that money. Counted on that money to save his father's restaurant before he returned.

He'd had a weak moment when he lent the money to the professor, but at the time he had liked and believed in the man. Jonathan was a regular at his restaurant and he'd

gotten caught up in the man's life. With his own father
absent, Jack somehow felt a closeness to the professor. He
was a man with a dream, something Jack had abandoned
years ago. He respected Jonathan for that and somehow he
wanted to be a part of that dream. He felt by helping him,
he could make amends for the things he'd done in the past.
He had also hoped he could better himself, better his
father's restaurant and do something his father would be
proud of for the first time in his life.

Jack ran a hand through his dark hair, just wondering
what the king of the eatery world would say when he
returned and found out his reputation had been ruined by
his only son. That his own son had turned him from prince
to pauper in his absence. A son who'd do anything to
please the man he idolized. But now Jack realized, you
can't set up your hopes for the future by buying into someone else's dream.

"C'mon, Elliot. He had to have something stashed
away. Some kind of money or some piece of Incan treasure. Find it for me. I want it. It's the only thing that can save
my ass now."

"Well, it seems he did have one Incan treasure hidden
away, Jack. And just as you wished, it's going to be yours."

"I knew it!" Jack's spirits lifted. The professor must have
found some Incan treasure before he kicked the bucket,
and left it to Jack to make up for losing his money. His life
wasn't turning so sour after all.

"This is great," said Jack. "Now I can sell the artifact and
use the money to save the restaurant. I should be able to

get the place in shape before my father returns, don't you think?"

"You can't sell this treasure, Jack."

"Sure I can. Everything has its price. Where is this precious piece anyway? I can't wait to get my hands on it."

The prayer service ended, and the few mourners who had showed up walked slowly back to their cars.

"Right there." Elliot pointed toward the gravesite.

"Right where?" Jack's eyes followed Elliot's finger.

"She's standing right next to the old lady and the priest."

"She?"

Jack's heart skipped a beat, and he removed his sunglasses and surveyed a young golden-skinned woman. She stood next to the priest and old lady who seemed to be comforting her. He couldn't have heard Elliot right. There was no way . . .

"Her name is Eden Ramirez. She's Professor Starke's Incan daughter," said Elliot as Jack looked on in shock.

The woman's back was toward him, and he couldn't help but think she looked ridiculous in the long, heavy orange skirt that reached down to her ankles and sandaled feet. She wore a short bright-red jacket which totally clashed and looked hotter than hell. It was a warm spring day, and the woman had to be uncomfortable dressed in all those layers of fabric. She had some sort of white tall hat with a black band around it upon her head—one of the most hideous things he'd ever seen. Her long ebony-black braids were thick and tied together in back with a vibrant green ribbon. She had some sort of brightly colored striped cloth flung across her shoulders like a back pack. It was mostly hot pink, making Jack's eyes hurt just to look at it. The material bulged as if she carried her belongings in it. The woman stuck out like a sore thumb, and Jack couldn't believe he hadn't even noticed her until Elliot pointed her out.

"What do you mean she's going to be mine?" Jack spoke in a low monotone, pushing the words from his lips, forcing them to go.

"Seems the professor spent his last penny on a plane ticket to fly her from the Andes to be at his side when he died. A one-way ticket, so she's stuck here. She doesn't have any money and has nowhere to stay."

"Not my problem." Jack twirled his mirrored sunglasses in his hand, then slapped them back on his face and headed for the car.

"Seems it is your problem, Jack." Elliot followed close on his heels. "The old lady who was the professor's neighbor said he told her to go to you. That you'd help her. Help her get home."

"Like hell. I'm not dishing out any more money. Especially for a plane ticket to Peru. And why did he think I'd help her after what he did to me?" Jack jumped in the car, turned the key, and revved the engine. "Just tell the little girl that I'm sorry I couldn't help."

"Maybe you'd like to tell her yourself. Here she comes now."

Jack looked up to see the priest waving him down from across the lawn. He and the old woman guided the girl toward him. If he stepped on the gas now he could make it to the front gates before they got to the car. He toyed with the idea and looked back to Elliot who had a smirk on his face.

"Damn it, Elliot, wipe that smirk off your face. My restaurant is going broke, my father's coming home in a few short months, and now I find out I'm getting a girl instead of my money and all you can do is stand there and grin!"

"If you hurry, Jack, you might be able to get out of here before she makes it to the car."

"Not a bad idea." Jack jammed the gear into drive just as he heard the priest call out to him.

"God bless you, Jack Talon, for taking this lost child into your care. You are like God's shepherd guiding the lost lamb."

Jack took a slow breath and released it. Why did the priest have to put it that way? He never could turn away someone in need. And that always got him in trouble.

Instead of speeding away like he wanted to, he slowly put the car into park and turned off the ignition. Lost lamb, the priest had called her. He doubted it. If she was anything like her father, she was probably a wolf in sheep's clothing. She'd probably be after whatever little money he had left. But still, he couldn't leave the girl all alone in a foreign land. It wouldn't kill him to give her a place to sleep and some bread and water until Elliot found some long lost relative of the professor's to take care of her.

"God will smile on you for this," whispered Elliot from the curb as the threesome came nearer.

"Yeah, well, if I ever meet God face to face, he'd better smile," grumbled Jack. "And when my father gets home and kills me for losing everything he's worked so hard for, and finds out I've ruined his name, I may just have that chance of meeting the creator face to face after all."

"Or his competition." Elliot smiled, looking like the devil himself.

"Just see what you can do about getting me out of this mess," ordered Jack. "I'll keep the girl at my place for a few days while you pull some ropes."

"And what ropes might those be?" asked Elliot, squinting in the sun as he spoke.

"The ropes that'll make up your noose if you leave me in this mess."

"My hands are tied, Jack. There's nothing I can do. I'm a private investigator, not some sort of magician."

"What do you mean by that? There's gotta be someone who'll take the professor's daughter. He's got to have some kind of relative or—"

"There's no one, Jack. Why the hell do you think he sent the girl to you?"

"To sell off as a slave to pay back the money he owes me?"

"Oooh, I wouldn't talk that way if I were you. A man who's wanting the good Lord to smile on him and all."

Jack winced as the trio approached his convertible. A trusting priest, a feeble old woman, and an overdressed circus girl with a hat so big it cast shadows over her face. What was he getting himself into? Why hadn't he just driven out of this place while he still had the chance?

"I no longer give a damn about anyone smiling on me," grumbled Jack to himself as he waved a pretense greeting toward the priest and flashed a fake smile. The only one he needed smiling on him right now was Lady Luck herself.

Chapter 2

Eden peeked out from under her hat at the handsome man behind the steering wheel of a small car. Father Elswood blessed himself and then laid his hands atop her shoulders in what she figured was another blessing.

Before she knew it, Mrs. Hammond, her father's neighbor, was opening the door and helping her get into the vehicle.

"Where are we going?" she said in her own language, forgetting the Americans had no idea what she was saying. She'd been so flustered lately, that it was taking her awhile to decipher their English words. But she did understand the name Jack Talon, and that this was the man her father had instructed her to go to for help.

The car sped off with her in it. Her glance at the side mirror showed Father Elswood and Mrs. Hammond waving a slow good-bye. A click and loud music coming from the radio dragged her attention back to the man named Jack as they zipped away.

She kept her head down, not sure what to do, not knowing what to say. She was alone in this strange country with no one to care for her. Her father was dead, and her mother waited for her back home.

The man named Jack didn't speak at all, and this made her nervous. She peeked up from under the brim of her hat and observed the man behind the wheel. The sun beamed down atop his neatly trimmed dark hair. His sideburns lowered to just in front of the ears. His hair ended just above the collar. All perfect. Not a hair out of place.

He wore a pair of mirrored sunglasses which kept her from seeing the color of his eyes. He had a strong nose and a mouth that looked as if it'd be good for kissing—something she'd never experienced but longed to try. He was clean shaven with a dimple in the middle of his chin that made him even more striking.

He wore a white pinstriped satin shirt and a black suit that looked as if it was expensive. By the frown on his face, she was sure he was feeling as much grief over her father's death as she was.

She didn't know how Jack was acquainted with her father but knew he must have been a close friend if her father placed her in Jack's care.

She felt safe with him. Sure of him. She knew he would help her return home to her mother and relatives, and she knew he would pay for her ticket. After all, he looked as if he could afford it. Her family was poor. They farmed the land for a living. They wove their own clothes, grew their own food, and even built their own houses—whatever they needed to do to survive. They'd learned to live on little and had never wanted anyone's help. That is, she'd never wanted anyone's help before now.

Jack couldn't help feeling the hairs on the back of his neck prickle the way this woman was staring at him. She made him nervous for some odd reason. She'd been riding in the car for a good ten minutes and still hadn't said a word. The least she could say was thank you. After all, he was under no obligation to help her out. Matter of fact, he wasn't sure why he was doing this.

He glanced at her, and she looked away quickly. He pulled up to a stoplight and reached over her lap to pop the glove compartment open. She lurched toward the door, and he realized he must have scared her.

"Only trying to get my smokes." He pulled out the pack of cigarettes and slammed the glove compartment closed. Gee, the girl was jumpy. He ripped open the package with his teeth and tapped a cigarette into his palm. He caught her looking at him again and offered her the package. "Care for one?"

She looked at the package and then back down to the floor.

"Guess not." He pushed in the lighter, thinking this whole thing was a big mistake. "So." He really didn't know what to say. "Sorry to hear your father didn't have the money to send you back home."

Somehow that didn't sound the way he'd intended it to. She crossed her hands over her chest and lowered that damned big hat of hers like she was taking a siesta. He pulled out the lighter, lit the cigarette, and pushed the lighter back in place. She was peeking at him again, probably not knowing what the hell a cigarette lighter was, now that he thought about it.

"It's a lighter. It makes fire." He talked slow and deliberate, trying to make conversation but seeing she didn't understand. "Great! You don't even speak English." He blew out a puff of smoke and took off in a squeal when the light turned green. "Just what I need. The swindling souse kicks the bucket and leaves me strapped with a child that can't say boo. Hell, she probably speaks Spanish," he said out loud. "Too damned bad I never learned it."

Eden bit her lip, wanting to curse at him in his native language. She understood him perfectly. It was all coming back to her after being here and hearing the English language for a few days now. Not to mention that he was talking slowly, which made it a bit easier. Well, she wasn't going to give him the benefit of knowing she understood him. Not after he called her father a swindling souse and her a child. Let him stew in whatever it was that was eating him. She'd tell him in due time she knew what he was saying, but for now she'd let him suffer a bit. She was in no mood for talking at the moment, so this scenario suited her fine. Plus by keeping quiet, she would find out exactly what Jack Talon really thought of her father. She wanted to find out before she gave him the contents of the bag to pay off her father's debt.

They pulled up in front of a restaurant. The lighted sign atop the building read The Golden Talon. There wasn't an empty parking space on the street, and he squealed the tires as he rounded the corner and pulled into an alleyway out back. He pushed a button, and a garage door automatically opened. He barreled into the three-car garage and came to a sudden stop. He shut off the motor and hopped from the car.

"You coming, or what?"

She knew she couldn't stay there all day so decided to follow him. She was no sooner out of the car than he had the garage door coming down, and she had to run to make it out before it closed. She scanned the grounds as she followed on his heels to the back of the restaurant. A row of tall pine trees made a natural barrier to a parking lot that sat just on the other side of the restaurant.

The yard itself was small, but green. Mostly weeds, some trees. Lots of sun, but no flowers or vegetable garden anywhere. A domed glass room sat atop the restaurant, and she wondered what it was.

She followed him through the back of the building, which was a large kitchen. Two men in white aprons were tossing dough in the air between them. People buzzed around her carrying trays of food. One woman stood at a metal counter making salads, and a big man with a crooked jaw hosed down dirty dishes and loaded them into a machine.

Jack stopped for a second and grabbed a steak off a waitress's tray. "Who the hell cooked this?" he asked.

The waitress nodded with her head to the short Mexican by the grills.

"Alfredo, you killed the cow again. Did the customer say they wanted their steak burnt?"

"No burnt. That's medium."

"Like hell. Try it again and do it right this time. I don't want any complaints. Rare is still mooing, medium is red and runny, and well done is pink. How many times do I have to tell you? That's the way my father's always done it."

As Jack walked through the kitchen, Eden heard Alfredo tell his co-worker in Spanish that he'd done it on purpose since he was upset that Jack didn't give him the raise in salary he'd been promised over three months ago. His co-worker nodded and said they were all upset with the way Jack was treating them lately. He himself had put a dead cricket atop one of the customer's salads.

Eden could feel the stares on her as she made her way through the swinging doors and out into the semi-empty restaurant. She caught sight of Jack sliding into a booth and heard him calling to a waitress.

"Ruthie, bring me a coffee and my phone."

"Right away, Jack."

"And tell Nathan to get over here. I need to talk to him."

Eden eyed the restaurant. Big. Fancy. Clean. Lots of tables but not lots of customers for so near the noon time hour. She didn't wonder why, when people like Alfredo and his co-worker were sabotaging the business. But then again, if Jack had treated them better maybe they wouldn't stoop to such low tricks.

She sat on a bar stool instead of joining Jack at the booth. She could see the curl of his cigarette smoke rising far above the padded seats even though she couldn't see his head. The waitress named Ruthie brought him a whole pot of coffee and a portable phone. He then was joined by the man named Nathan who she guessed, helped run the place.

"What do you mean—don't put in the meat order? What are we going to feed the customers?"

"I don't know," snapped Jack. "Think of a way to handle it. Put less meat and more fillers in the meatballs. You think of how to pull it off. I can't afford it this week. I was counting on some money that never came. I need to pay the electric bill or they're going to shut us off."

"What about the refrigerators? They're on the blink again."

"See if you can get one of the cooks to try and fix them."

"You can't be serious? What do they know? Can I tell them that you'll pay overtime?"

"Hell no. Get Alfredo to fix them. He can't cook anyway. Rafael can double up on the chores."

"What'll it be, ma'am?"

Eden looked up to see Ruthie standing before her chomping on a piece of gum. A woman in her fifties with a wad of gum just didn't seem right to Eden.

"Did you want to order, or are you just going to sit there and stare?"

"She can't talk," came Jack's voice from the booth. The phone was on his ear and he spoke into it and to Ruthie on and off.

"Whad'ya mean she can't talk? And what's up with these rags she's wearing? Is she one of them bums from the streets? I thought you stopped letting beggars in here, Jack."

What a rude woman. No wonder there weren't any customers. If she spoke like that to all Jack's customers, they'd run from here in a hurry.

She was about to give Ruthie her order when Jack called out, "She's from Peru. Speaks Spanish I think. See if you can get Alfredo to ask her what she wants. Oh hell, just bring her whatever we have left over."

Eden hated this place already. And she now knew where Ruthie got her rudeness lessons. Jack wasn't high on the ladder of winning personalities either. Why bother to talk when Jack Talon had already made up his mind she couldn't, and was doing it for her? Eden decided she'd sit back and let Jack act like a fool. He deserved it. She'd let him think she couldn't speak English—for now. She'd tell him when she darned well felt like it.

She took the menu and smiled. She pointed to the potato soup and then handed the menu back to Ruthie.

"Soup, huh?" Ruthie chomped on her gum. "You probably don't even know what you ordered, you poor thing. I'll bring you a hamburger."

"Bring her the soup," called Jack, and Eden was amazed how he could hear their conversation, talk on the phone, and talk to Nathan all at once. "We've got to save the meat for the dinner crowd. We're running low."

Her impression of him being a generous, caring man was changing rapidly. She ate her soup in silence and sipped on the lemon tinged water. She watched Jack from under the brim of her hat as he talked to Nathan and at the same time shouted instructions to the employees, more or less scaring the hell out of her every time he raised his voice. She picked up her water and went over to sit at a table by the window. She didn't like being in such closed quarters and longed for the open skies of home.

Passersby stopped and stared at her brightly colored clothes, and she smiled at them and waved, just trying to be friendly. Before she knew it, a dozen people entered the restaurant, if nothing else just because they were curious about her.

"Jack, do you want me to stay on till the dinner shift?" asked Ruthie.

Jack glanced up from his phone call and noticed the people in the restaurant. This was the first time in the last six months he had customers between lunch and dinner. What was happening here?

"Where'd all the people come from?" He motioned for Nathan to leave the booth and get back to work.

"She brought them in." Ruthie popped a bubble.

"She? She who?"

"The circus girl."

Jack peered over the top of the booth and noticed Eden sitting right near the window. He cringed and hung up on his phone call and jumped from the booth with the phone still in his hand.

"How long has she been sitting there in prime view?"

"Long enough for half the city to see her."

"Damn! This isn't some kind of side show. Get her out of there and take her upstairs."

"Whatever you say. But who's going to wait on the tables?"

Jack shook his head and placed the phone down on the table. "Forget it. I'll handle this myself." He stormed over to the window seat, smiling politely to the customers on the way. "Come with me, little Miss Muffet." He grabbed her arm and pulled her along behind him as he made his way up the stairs.

"Eden," she corrected him.

He stopped in his tracks and stared at the top of her ridiculous hat. Well, she knew her name anyway, though he was certain she had no idea of what he was saying.

"Eden," he ground out and headed up the stairs.

Chapter 3

When Jack opened the door to the room, Eden couldn't believe her eyes. It was a huge apartment, bigger than three of their houses put together back home. And the sky—the beautiful sky lit up the room through the wonderful glass-domed ceiling overhead.

"I guess you'll have to stay here. It's my place, but I don't know where else to put you."

As she marveled the place over, Jack spoke slow and childlike again trying to make her understand. Gee, was he going to feel stupid when she decided to respond in English.

"Home. You stay here." He walked over to the huge bed and patted his hand on the quilted comforter atop. "Bed." He then walked over to a door and pointed at it. "Bathroom."

He was irritating her to no end with his absurd way of talking, but she still kept quiet since she knew she was irritating him more.

"And take off that damned hat already."

When she did nothing to remove it, he walked over and plucked it from her head, throwing it into the wicker chair that stood next to a glass and rattan dinette table.

For a brief moment she froze. She'd never felt so naked in her entire life without the security of her hat. And he'd plucked it from her head effortlessly as if he was plucking a berry from the vine. Her eyes met his and she found herself staring, unable to pull her gaze away. She now knew the color of his eyes perfectly. Azure blue like the skies that blanketed the mountains of Cuzco. The brilliant color didn't fit him. She'd figured he had cold, stark eyes of ebony with the personality he carried. Instead they were bright, warm, understanding and forgiving all at the same time.

His bushy brows danced as he surveyed her face. "Not quite the child I had you pegged for, are you? You've got quite a pretty face."

She could feel herself blushing but wouldn't look away. If she did, she'd give herself away that she understood what he was saying. Instead, she held her gaze steady, sure she could out-stare him if she tried.

"You shouldn't hide that pretty face under such an ugly hat." His gaze traveled down her body, and she was thankful she was well covered at the moment. Still, his sweeping perusal made her feel as if she was standing there stark naked.

She was waiting for his next compliment, enjoying the fact he didn't know she understood his language, or he probably would never be saying these things. Still, she liked to hear them.

"I bet you have quite a body under all those clothes."

She felt the heat rising inside her.

"I hear those mountain women are built like horses."

She blinked as he stepped away, not believing what she'd just heard.

"Of course," he added as he headed across the room, "I also hear they have the stamina during sex to keep a man fully pleased."

She didn't dare look at him after that comment. Right about now she wanted to tell him exactly what she thought of him. And if she wasn't so tongue-tied she probably would have.

"I'm so glad you can't understand a word I'm saying. It's so nice not to have to pretend around a woman. He came closer to her, sniffed and crinkled his nose. You smell like . . . llama." He spit the words off his tongue. "How 'bout a bath?"

She bit her tongue and turned around slowly. She'd never in her life met such an arrogant, rude man. When she turned back around she realized he was already in the bathroom filling the tub with water. She walked over and peered into the room.

"Bath," he over pronounced as she stood in the door-way.

"Bath," she repeated with a stiff upper lip.

"That's right. You're learning. A couple words a day and we should be able to converse in about a year or two."

Jack headed out the door, swearing he heard her saying "bastard" as he left the room. Impossible. She must have been practicing the word bath and was saying it wrong. He'd have to work with her on that one.

Chapter 4

The dinner rush ended, and Jack sat down with his tenth cup of coffee and second pack of cigarettes that day.

"Where the hell did that rush come from, Ruthie?" he asked his waitress as she sat across from him counting her tips.

"I told you it was that circus girl you brought in here. I don't know where you dug her up, but it really worked."

"She's not a circus girl. I told you, she's from Peru. She's the professor's daughter. She'll be staying with us for a while."

"Professor Starke? I thought you had it in for him. Doesn't he owe you lots of money or something?"

"He's dead. His funeral was today." Jack took a deep drag of the cigarette and blew the smoke in the air.

"So what's his daughter doing here then?"

"I don't know," snapped Jack. "The old man told her I'd take care of her for some strange reason. What a notion."

Ruthie took the gum from her mouth, and stuck it in the ashtray. "So are you going to send her back to the mountains or what?"

He took another drag and blew it out.

"How the hell should I know? I have enough problems to think about for now. Plus I can't afford to send her back."

"Can't—or won't? Seems to me you have a soft spot somewhere in that black heart of yours or you never would have taken her in to begin with."

"You're full of nonsense, Ruthie. The whole thing just caught me off guard."

"You used to be a real lover, Jack. Maybe you need a little lady around here to soften you up again. No one can stand you since you broke up with Ginny. Maybe you just need a good lay and you'd stop being such a bastard."

"Ruthie, anyone but you and I wouldn't put up with that kind of talk. You'd be outta here on your ass."

"Seems to me, your ass is the one on the line with your father coming back so soon. Once he sees what's happened to his restaurant, he's going to kill you with that temper of his."

"Don't remind me. I never should have lent the money to that fluke of a professor. I've totally let my father down. Once he finds out I've wrecked the family business, I'll be out on the streets like little Miss Muffet upstairs, with nowhere to go. I blew it, Ruthie. I was never cut out for this business. I never wanted to do it in the first place. I'm a twenty-six-year-old high school drop out without a diploma and soon to be without a job."

"You could always go back to school."

"Bite your tongue, Ruthie. I'm too damned old for that. I screwed up early in life, and my father's the only one who's given me a chance. All I wanted to do was show him I'm capable of running a business and making it succeed without the proper schooling."

"You were doing fine, Jack."

"Fine until I met Professor Jonathan Starke. He's taken me for a ride and left me without a pot to piss in."

"Oh, I don't know about that, Jack. After all, he did leave you his most precious possession. He left you his daughter. Maybe you shouldn't be so hard on the little lady. After all, she did bring in quite a crowd this afternoon. I rather like seeing the tip money again."

"No little lady is going to change anything around here, Ruthie. And the one upstairs is definitely not Lady Luck. More like Lady Disaster. It was a fluke we got busy today. It had nothing to do with her. And I won't have her sitting in the window like a side show in that get-up anymore. Do me a favor and take her shopping or something. Buy her some clothes so she can blend in a little better and not make me the town gossip on tomorrow's paper. I've got to build up the reputation of this restaurant the way it was before I let it slip. I've got to think of something to save this place and fast."

Jack walked through the kitchen, feeling like he could have been a little nicer to Eden. After all, it wasn't her fault her father had ruined his life. He walked up to one of the wall refrigerators and pulled it open. He pulled out a piece of cherry pie and realized it wasn't as cold as it should be.

"Alfredo. Did you get a chance to look at these refrigerators yet?"

"No, Señor Talon. The crowd took us by surprise."

"Can you stay late and . . . "

"No stay. I've got to get home to feed the dog."

Jack knew Alfredo wouldn't stay unless he paid extra but he just couldn't afford it right now.

"All right. Empty this fridge into the ones that work halfway decent and we'll take a look at it tomorrow."

"Sí, Señor Talon."

"And quit calling me Señor Talon. My name's Jack, so use it."

Alfredo grunted.

"By the way, I was wondering if you could teach me a couple words in Spanish."

"Why for?"

"I want to be able to talk with Eden."

"Does she speak Spanish, Señor Jack?"

"How the hell should I know? Isn't that what they speak over in that part of the world?"

Alfredo mumbled something in Spanish under his breath.

"What does that mean?" asked Jack.

"It means we'll start on the lessons in the morning."

Somehow he knew better but let it slide. He picked up a clean fork and the cherry pie and headed upstairs. He figured he'd bring Eden some dessert, and hopefully they could start all over. Even if she had no idea of the way he'd talked to her, it still tugged at his conscience a little.

It was late and already dark. He figured she'd be sleeping so he opened the door quietly. The night stars shone brightly through the glass-domed ceiling, the full moon lighting up the darkened room with a soft bluish glow.

Her clothes and that silly hat lay atop his bed, but she was nowhere to be seen. He set the pie on the glass table and made his way over to the table lamp. He switched it on and the light engulfed the room. His gaze swept the place, and he realized she could only be in the one room with a door in the open apartment. The bathroom.

He called her name but heard no answer. The door was ajar and he pushed it open, switching on the light as he did so. It was then that he realized she had never gotten out of the bathtub. Instead she had fallen asleep.

The light woke her up and she sat upright, her long unbound hair falling around her shoulders. He couldn't stop his eyes from wandering to her high, perky breasts. She was certainly not the child he'd first thought she was. Her dusky nipples were standing out straight on her bronze skin and he felt himself stirring below his belt.

It had been a long time since he'd had a woman. Ginny had left him to go live abroad, and he took it personally, delving instead into his work. Work and bad investments from having a weary mind.

Eden blinked in the bright light trying to catch her bearings. She rose to her feet, splashing water over the side of the tub. Without even realizing it, she was getting Jack more aroused than he'd ever allowed himself to get since Ginny dumped him.

He swallowed hard, not able to speak. The woman under all those silly clothes was beautiful. Her stomach was tight and lean, her hips were well rounded but nothing like the huge hips he had imagined. At the juncture of her thighs was a black triangle of silken curls. Curls he longed to run his hand through. And she had strong, shapely legs he'd love to feel wrapped around his hips.

Then she screamed and grabbed a towel to hide her beauty and deny him the wonders God had given her. He closed his eyes and backed out the door.

Damn! How careless of him to enter and not remember she was in the tub. But still, he had called her name and she hadn't answered. Then again, she'd only said two words since he met her. He'd come up to try to make things right and instead he'd made them worse.

He walked over to the closet and pulled out one of his dress shirts. He threw it on the bed, all the while keeping his back to the bathroom door.

"Ruthie's going to take you shopping tomorrow. I'll give her some money. For now you can wear one of my shirts to sleep in."

What the hell was he doing? She couldn't understand a word he was saying. She probably thought he was waiting for her to come out so he could take her to bed. He couldn't blame her. It did seem that way. And just the thought of it excited him more. He had to get out of there, though he had nowhere to go.

He'd given her his place to use, and now he couldn't trust himself in the same room with her all night. Not after seeing her naked. He'd never sleep when he was so aroused.

"Eden!" he called, but knew she'd never come out of the bathroom as long as he was still here. "Eden, I'm leaving now and won't be back until morning. I know you can't understand me—but . . . but I wanted to say . . . I'm sorry. I'm sorry about your father, and I'm sorry about being such a jerk."

Eden heard his words clearly from the bathroom and also the slam of the door and his footsteps going down the stairs. She opened the door carefully and peeked around, just to be sure. The room of glass was now covered by purple velvet curtains that encompassed the entire room. He must have closed them for her privacy before he left.

She tiptoed out to the bed and picked up her old clothes. They were dirty and she now realized they did smell like llama. Alpaca to be exact. She missed the furry animals, and she missed the mountains of home. She felt so fresh and clean now that she dreaded the thought of putting her alpaca wool clothes back on. Then she saw the shirt he'd left for her on the bed.

She picked it up in one hand reveling in the silken softness. Such luxury to be able to wear such expensive threads so close to her bare skin. She rubbed it against her face and couldn't help but notice that it smelled like his cologne. She closed her eyes and took a deep breath. She couldn't wear this without dreaming of him.

She wouldn't wear this—even if he did say he was sorry. He was a rude man, and she wanted nothing to do with him. He obviously didn't like her father much and it was no secret that he didn't like her.

She had never felt so alone in her life. Her mother and family were hundreds of miles away, her father dead. She was a foreigner in a strange land of rude people. She had no one to talk to, no one to tell of the grief that was eating her up from the inside out. If only she could allow herself to cry—but she wouldn't.

She pulled down the comforter and eyed the beautiful leopard-skin sheets. It reminded her of the ocelot that roamed wild in the jungles of the Amazon. It also reminded her of the man whose bed she'd be sleeping in that night. She lay down naked, wondering where he would spend the night. Probably in the arms of a woman somewhere. Suddenly she felt a strange pang in the area of her heart. She pulled the sheets up over her and lay on her back looking at the stars beyond the glass-domed ceiling.

What if she were that woman he spent the night with? A strange part of her longed to know how it would feel. She shoved the thought from her mind and instead focused on the few stars she could see in the skies.

In the Andes the nights were so dark you could see the stars by the millions. Here, you were lucky to see the moon and the big dipper. She fell asleep wondering if North Americans thought they were lucky to see these stars. Then she wondered if they ever really even saw them at all.

Chapter 5

Jack was in the middle of an erotic dream with a scantily dressed circus girl when a hand on his shoulder woke him up. He almost jumped through the ceiling when he opened his eyes and instead of the curvaceous girl of his dreams an ugly motorcyclist with tattoos stood before him.

"Damn it, Nathan. What the hell are you doing with your hands on me?"

"It's morning and it's time we open for breakfast. What the hell you doin' sleeping in the booth anyway?"

It was then that Jack remembered he'd spent the night in the booth as Eden was occupying his bed. He had a kink in his neck and morning mouth. He needed a shave and a quick shower. He pushed himself from the booth and stretched. Latisha, his African-American waitress, very pregnant with her fourth child, walked up to him and handed him his morning coffee and a pack of cigarettes.

"I hear you're entertaining a circus girl now-a-days."

He blinked, then recognized the connection between his erotic dream and seeing Eden naked last night.

"What the hell is this? Talk time with Tisha? Don't you have tables to set? Get to work."

She rubbed her big belly and smiled. "Don't do anything I wouldn't do."

"A comforting thought. I don't make such mistakes."

"This wasn't a mistake. And don't forget, I'm married."

Married she was. But hell if anyone knew where her drunken husband had disappeared to. The girl was only twenty-two years old and already on her fourth kid. If it wasn't for him giving her work, she and the kids would have starved by now. And he didn't know what he was going to tell her when he had to let her go any day because he couldn't afford to keep her on.

"Where's the kids today, Tisha?" Jack groaned and rubbed his face in his hands.

"I sent them upstairs to watch TV like I always do when I'm working. Why?"

"Oh shit. You didn't."

"Jack, what's the matter with you? If you don't want the kids trashing the place, then just tell me and I'll find somewhere else to put them while I'm doing my shift."

"No, no, Tisha. It's not that. It's just—oh never mind. Nathan, open the restaurant and see to it that Alfredo looks at the refrigerators. I've got to get upstairs, quick."

Jack ran up the stairs and threw open the door expecting to find Eden cowering in the corner, screaming because three wild kids had stormed in on her while she was sleeping.

Instead, he found something that took him by surprise. Eden, fully clothed in her dress and sandals sat on the bed with little three-year-old Patsy in her lap. Six-year-old Randal sat backwards on a chair in front of her and the eighteen-month-old Nicola crawled around exploring the floor.

They were laughing when he opened the door but the laughter ceased as soon as they all saw him.

"Well, I see you met Tisha's kids." By habit he walked over to the curtains. It was then that he realized they were already opened. Not only that, but an empty wine bottle sat on the table with a bunch of blooming weeds in it, right next to the empty and washed plate that had held the cherry pie he'd brought her last night.

"Guess you were up early today."

"Eden's nice," said little Patsy.

"Yeah," agreed Randal. "We like her a lot."

"How'd you know her name?" asked Jack.

Randal opened his mouth, then closed it when Eden looked at him. Jack didn't know what the hell was going on.

"She told us," said Patsy.

"Yeah, well, that's all she can say, so get used to it, kids." Jack walked over and picked up the youngest who was now exploring the inside of his closet. "Eden's from a different part of the world and can't talk like we talk."

"I want to go to Peru when I grow up." Randal smiled.

"Peru? That's a big word for such a little boy. Did she tell you she was from there?"

"Peru." Eden spoke before Randal could answer. "Peru," she repeated slowly.

Jack handed the baby to Randal and helped Patsy get off Eden's lap.

"Why don't you kids go down to the kitchen and see if Rafael can cook you up some eggs."

"Rafael's here?" asked Randal excitedly. "I thought you told him not to come in anymore before lunchtime."

Damn. That was right. He had to cut the man's hours last week. Rafael was good with the kids, and Jack just wanted a few minutes alone with Eden before he took a shower and changed.

"Then go ask Alfredo to cook you some eggs, but tell him not to burn them. And when you're done, go play in the yard. Alfredo's got a refrigerator to fix, so don't be slowing him down."

"Okay, Mr. Talon." Randal carried the baby on his hip and took Patsy by the hand. "Good-bye Eden. I hope you'll be here tomorrow so we can see you again."

She didn't answer, just waved her hand as they left.

There was an awkward moment when the door closed and Jack and Eden were left alone in the room. Silence. As always. The damned silence was really starting to get to him. Right about now he'd give anything just to have a conversation.

"Well." He flashed a smile. "I take it you slept good in my bed?"

She lowered her head as always, and if he didn't know better he'd say she was embarrassed. She must know the word bed, Jack figured. Probably thought he was asking her to join him.

"Look, I've got to take a shower. Bath," he added and pointed toward the door for her sake.

She backed away slightly, her eyes wide. Probably figured he was telling her to take another bath. Two baths in one month was most likely unheard of in her part of the world.

He started unbuttoning his shirt, and she turned away. When he took it off and flung it over the back of the chair, he realized she'd donned that damned hat of hers again and was staring out the window. He walked over to her and was reaching out to pluck it from her head when she turned abruptly and grabbed his wrist before he could remove the silly thing.

"You've got a strong grip."

She didn't say anything, as usual, just held his wrist and looked into his eyes. Jack found himself lost in her big blue eyes. Eyes that were American, not Peruvian at all. Eyes that reminded him of Professor Jonathan Starke. They were truly windows to her soul. He swore he could see her whole life reflected in them. Innocence, hurt, abandonment, confusion, and most of all a depth to a woman he wanted to know better.

He reached out with his other hand, placed it around her fingers, and loosened her grip. "Oh, all right. Keep the hat on. For now. Ruthie's taking you shopping this morning, and I want you to pick out something a little less frumpy if possible."

"Frumpy," she said and walked across the room.

"Yeah, frumpy. It means—oh hell, you wouldn't understand."

There was a knock at the door, and he went over to open it. Ruthie stood there chomping on a piece of gum, her eyes scanning his half naked body and then looking across the room at Eden.

"Sorry to interrupt. Maybe I should come back later?"

"Don't start with me, Ruthie." He dug in his back pocket and pulled out his wallet. He handed her his American Express card.

"Buy her something a little more—something that'll make her look a little less—"

"Frumpy," Eden repeated as she walked up to Ruthie.

Ruthie cocked an eyebrow at Jack.

"She learned a new word today," he said.

"You teaching her English?"

"Not really. Probably too hard for her to understand. Instead, Alfredo's going to teach me a few phrases in Spanish so I can try to communicate with the girl."

Ruthie snapped her gum and eyed up Eden. "I see. So, how much do you want me to spend on her?"

"Whatever it takes." He ran a hand through his hair and yawned. "No, actually, you'd better keep it to two outfits and a nightgown. I've got to start cutting back."

"Two outfits? A girl can't live on that!" Ruthie was aghast.

"She's not staying here long if I can help it. This is only to tide her over till I can think of what to do with her."

"Whatever you say, boss. I'll be back for the lunch rush."

"There won't be another rush. Yesterday was a fluke."

"Too bad. I could use the money. That is, an extra ten or twenty would be helpful around now as I really could use a new pair of shoes and some more gum."

"Put it on the charge, Ruthie. Just don't get carried away."

"Thanks, boss." Ruthie took Eden by the hand. "C'mon sweetie. We'll doll you up real pretty. You'll look so good Jack won't want to get rid of you."

Jack closed the door and leaned his head against it. Somehow he had a feeling Ruthie would do just that. And somehow he knew she was always right. But the last thing he needed in his life right now was a woman. Especially one who couldn't understand a word he was saying.

❦

"So. Where are we going?" asked Eden as soon as they'd gotten in the car and closed the door.

Ruthie looked at her, open mouthed. "You can talk. English, I mean."

"Of course." Eden pulled down the mirror on the visor and used it to straighten her hat. "Who said I couldn't?"

"Well—Jack did."

"Jack knows nothing."

"And you didn't want him to know, did you?"

Eden looked at her and smiled. "I like to listen to him talk like a child, hoping I'll understand. I like to hear him say things he wouldn't, if he thought I understood."

"You are a sly one, Eden."

"You won't tell?"

"I'll let you tell him, sweetie. I don't want to get into the middle of a domestic quarrel."

"Domestic quarrel?"

"Never mind. Now let's go shopping and get you something that'll drive Jack crazy."

"Ruthie, what do you mean by that?"

"I mean, the man's got the hots for you. He's giving you the eye. In other words, he likes you, Eden."

Eden felt her body tingle when Ruthie said the words. Did Jack really like her, or have the hots for her, as Ruthie said? She was sure he didn't, the way he talked down to her, called her clothes frumpy, and always wanted to rip off her hat. Still, the idea of such a handsome man liking her was appealing in a way. But then she remembered the way he had talked about her father and it angered her.

"Well, I don't like Mr. Talon," she said and slammed the mirror on the visor shut. "He's a rude man. Annoying."

"He's buying you clothes, honey, and letting you sleep in his bed while he sleeps downstairs in a booth. There really is some good in that man somewhere."

So, that was where he slept last night. Not in the arms of a woman. Eden knew Ruthie was right about him not being so bad, but didn't want to admit it. She wasn't sure about the whole situation, but only knew she wanted to get home.

"Is he sending me home, Ruthie?"

Ruthie started the motor and pulled out into traffic. "Do you want to leave already, sweetie?"

"Sí. I hate it here. I just want to get back to the mountains. To my people."

Ruthie snapped her gum and turned on the radio. "Then you'd better talk to Jack about it. I don't believe he plans on buying that ticket to South America."

"Will you ask him for me, Ruthie? Will you get him to buy my ticket?"

Ruthie shook her head and stepped on the gas.

"No, honey, that I won't do. I put in my two cents where it doesn't belong, but I respect Jack and his decisions. If you want him to send you home, then you're just going to have to ask him yourself."

Eden knew it was impossible to ask Jack to send her home without actually talking to him in English. She couldn't quite figure out Ruthie but had a feeling the woman said this purposely so she would have to talk to Jack. From what Eden had seen, Ruthie was probably the closest person to Jack around here. Ruthie said Jack liked her, though she couldn't see it herself. He really was handsome, and he did say he was sorry for being such a jerk. But still, he'd said things about her father she didn't like at all. No, she wasn't going to talk to him yet. That ticket back to Peru would just have to wait.

Chapter 6

It was well into the lunchtime hour when Eden and Ruthie returned from shopping. They came in through the open back door of the restaurant, almost running into Tisha's kids, who were playing hide and seek.

Eden grabbed Randal and bent down to whisper in his ear. "This is not a good place to play, Randal. Why don't you get your sisters and go into the yard for a while? It's a nice day."

"Okay." Randal smiled. "And then maybe we can talk some more later?"

"Perhaps. But remember our secret."

She winked at him and he winked back.

"Don't worry," whispered the boy. "I won't tell Mr. Talon you know how to talk."

She laughed and rearranged the manta, Peruvian shawl, on her back. The dress they had bought was in her manta. She had refused to wear the dress home. She wasn't even sure she liked the thing. But still, it would be a bit cooler than her own clothes.

"¡Hola!" greeted Alfredo, sticking his head out from behind the refrigeration unit.

Eden knew Spanish well, but she didn't feel like talking at the moment. She just wanted to get upstairs and take off her hot clothes. She greeted Alfredo in his own language, then explained she preferred to speak Quechua, her language.

"Well, then my little Spanish lesson with Jack this morning won't do him any good, will it?"

"Eden's tired," interrupted Ruthie, "so I'm sure she's anxious to get upstairs."

Eden smiled at her gratefully.

"So why are you not fixing lunch for the customers?" asked Ruthie.

"What customers? There's been so few this morning, I actually decided to look at the refrigerator because I was bored."

"Well, I'll go relieve Tisha so she can head on out then. Where's Jack?"

"Haven't seen him since we finished his meager Spanish lesson about an hour ago."

Eden headed out the swinging doors, waving to Tisha, who was standing near the register chatting with two women customers about to leave.

She picked up her skirt and started up the stairs to her new apartment. Jack's apartment. But still the only place she could hang her hat and call home at the moment. Thoughts of Jack ran through her head, and the way he'd frowned on her appearance. Who was he that he could judge so easily? There was nothing wrong with her clothing. It was perfectly acceptable—in Cuzco anyway.

She was rather appalled the way the American women ran around in little or nothing with their unbound breasts bobbing under their see-through tops, and their legs bared so high it left nothing to the imagination. Still, she thought they looked comfortable in those clothes. Chicago was muggy, and she was feeling as if she was ready to strip naked just to feel cooler.

She let herself into the room, closing the door quietly behind her. She walked over to the bed and tossed her hat down, followed by the manta on her back. Her belongings spilled out. The package she'd gotten today was followed by her hair brush, extra panties she'd brought on the trip, her passport, her panpipe, and then the burlap bag from her father and the Bible.

She picked up the Bible, holding it to her heart. How she missed her father and the way he read to her from this book every time he visited her land. He'd told her she was God's best creation. Just like the garden He had made for Adam and Eve. That's why her father and her mother decided to call her Eden.

She then placed the Bible gently on the bed and picked up the burlap bag. She'd almost forgotten about it. She didn't even know what was inside. Anxious and nervous, she pulled the rope tie and unfastened the bag. She paused, took a deep breath and fingered the locket with her father's photo that hung on the yarn around her neck. Bringing it to her mouth, she kissed it, then replaced it.

Her fingers reached out slowly as her hand entered the bag. Was it jewels he left? Was it money that she could use to help her get home? After all, he had said it was to be given to Jack to pay back some sort of debt. So whatever it was, it must be worth much.

"¡Hola!" came a voice from in the room behind her.

She jumped and turned around, the bag spilling its contents onto the ground.

"¿Cómo está usted?" she heard.

She spied Jack lounging on the couch across the room. His shirt was unbuttoned, and his shoes were off. His hair was tousled as if he'd been sleeping. He scared the hell out of her and she was angry. Why hadn't he made his presence known when she entered the room?

She cursed him out in her own language, telling him he should respect her privacy and other things that he obviously didn't understand—nor did she want him to.

"Oh, so you do have a tongue?"

He pushed himself off the couch, stretching and yawning as he did so.

"Didn't hear you come in, sweetie. I had a rough night sleeping and just thought I'd catch a few winks while the room was unoccupied."

She wondered why he hadn't used his own bed. Strange he'd choose the couch over the king-sized bed that sat there unoccupied at the time.

"So I see you went shopping. Let's see what you bought with my money. Dinero," he said with a proud smile on his face.

Eden wasn't surprised to see he had learned the Spanish word for money in his first lesson.

Jack headed over toward the bed, slipping on something but regaining his balance as he grabbed on to the back of the chair.

"What the hell is this?"

She watched him bend and scoop up a handful of something that must have fallen from the burlap bag. He held out his cupped palm for her to see.

"Is this yours?"

She let her eyes wander to his hand, her heart beating furiously, thinking he'd found her father's treasure and would now take it from her, when she wasn't even sure she wanted him to have it.

"Beans," he surveyed. "And some kind of seeds. Lots of them. Did you bring this with you? Yours?" he asked, pointing first to the seeds and then to her.

She almost answered him, wanting to tell him that her father gave them to her on his death bed, but now it all seemed so ridiculous. Instead, she shook her head no, and then thought about how important it had seemed to her father, and nodded her head yes.

"You really don't have a clue what I'm talking about, do you, you poor pathetic thing?"

She wanted to hit him at that moment. She wasn't pathetic. He was, with the way he spoke to her.

There was a knock at the door and he grabbed her hand, placing the seeds into it.

"Pick these up before someone gets hurt. Pick up." He motioned to the seeds scattered on the floor and then to her. He headed for the door, and she wished he was gone.

It was Ruthie, bless her soul. She'd come to her rescue. Eden didn't want to be alone with Jack any more than she had to. She was still embarrassed thinking he had seen her naked. No man had ever done that before, though she was old for a virgin in her part of the country.

"Jack, I thought I'd find you up here." Ruthie handed him his American Express card. "There's a man here to see you. Says he's the owner of the place across the street."

"What? That building's been empty for some time."

"I know." She slipped into the room and glanced toward Eden. "The man says he's the owner of the new restaurant they're opening there next week."

"New restaurant? What new restaurant? I don't need this kind of competition." He stormed out of the room.

Ruthie closed the door and looked at Eden. "Looks like he got you a bit shook up, hon. What's going on?"

Eden bent down to scoop up the seeds, gingerly placing them back in the burlap bag. She didn't like the fact that Ruthie could see her obvious emotions, though she tried well to hide them.

"Nothing he does can upset me, Ruthie. He just . . . caught me off guard."

Ruthie bent down next to her and helped her pick up the seeds.

"What are these?"

"Nothing important." Eden pulled the tie tight on the bag as she stood. What was happening to her? A minute ago she had thought what occupied the bag was very important. That is, until Jack made her question her values.

"Well." Ruthie stood and wiped her hands in her apron. "I have to get downstairs. My shift is starting, but I wanted to see that new dress on you first."

The new dress. Eden had almost forgotten about it. She put the seeds and Bible in the drawer, and picked up the bag that held her purchase. She opened it and held the dress in front of her. It was a brown-and-white-checkered house dress. Cotton, plain but cool. Much different from her own clothes or the vibrancy of their colors.

"I really wish you would have taken the dress I picked out for you, Eden."

"I don't think I like the one you picked out."

Ruthie plucked the hat from Eden's head, helping her undress.

"I hope this fits, since you refused to try it on at the store. Too modest to take your clothes off anywhere but at home, huh?"

Eden took off her saco, short jacket, and her uncu, long tunic shirt, and laid them on the bed. She was reaching for her skirt when she noticed Ruthie staring at her.

"Where's your bra, honey?"

Eden looked down at her bare breasts and all of a sudden wanted to cover up. It reminded her too much of when Jack had seen her naked. She never wore a bra in the mountains. Never had the need to as far as she was concerned. She grabbed the new dress and pulled it over her head even before removing her skirt.

"This dress is thin," commented Ruthie, helping her. "We should have gotten a slip for you to wear underneath it. And a bra, had I of known. Oh well, no matter. It'll have to do for now. Why don't you come downstairs with me, and we'll see what Jack thinks."

She didn't care what Jack thought about her dress, or at least she tried to convince herself of that fact. In actuality she was nervous and felt so naked without all the layers of clothes she was used to wearing. She still wore her sandals and grabbed her montera, native hat, and put it on her head. A little better at least.

"You're not going to wear that hat, are you?"

"I like my hat."

"Oh well, whatever. C'mon, I've got work to do."

She followed Ruthie downstairs. She could hear Jack talking even though she couldn't see him sitting in the booth. His trail of cigarette smoke rose lazily above the table and drifted out into the air.

"So you knew my father, Mr. Noble?" asked Jack.

"I know him," the man corrected. "And please, just call me Martin."

Ruthie disappeared into the kitchen and Eden, not knowing what to do, took a seat at the empty bar. She could see the back of Jack's head from where she was sitting and the face of the man across from him. The man looked noble, just like his name. He wore a tailored navy suit and a high buttoned collar with a thin tie. He had a well defined face and graying black hair. Eden guessed him to be in his mid fifties.

"Martin," she heard Jack say with contempt in his voice. "So you plan on opening The Ruby next week?"

"I do," he answered. "And you know I'm going to put you out of business."

Another puff of smoke lifted high over Jack's head and Eden couldn't help but think he was breathing fire like a dragon at the man's last comment.

"I'd like to see you try, Mr. Noble. The Golden Talon has been in the family for years. My father built this place up to the highest standards."

"And you let it fall to the lowest of lows," said Martin.

Jack rose at that comment and dunked his cigarette in the man's drink. "I'll have to ask you to leave before I become violent."

Martin Noble chuckled and got to his feet. His gold chains and Rolex sparkled in the artificial light. "And word on the street has it you would become violent, too, would-n't you, Jack?"

"If you don't get out of my sight fast, you're going to find out first hand."

"The Golden Talon has fallen, thanks to you, Jack. And I look forward to when your father returns and finds out his competition who put him out of business is the man he refused to hire when he first opened the place."

Eden watched a muscle twitch in Jack's jaw and his hand clench in a fist. Martin Noble turned on his heel and left. If he hadn't at that moment, Eden had no doubt Jack would have hit him. He ran his hand through his hair and grabbed the pack of cigarettes from the table. It was empty and he smashed it in his fingers and threw it down.

"What's the matter, boss?" Nathan walked up wiping his hands in a towel.

"Nothing I want to talk about at the moment." Jack stormed out through the kitchen.

Tisha walked through the swinging doors of the kitchen with a large tray in her hand. She smiled as she walked past Eden toward the table she was serving. The sound of a child crying in the distance brought her to a halt.

"That sounds like Nicola." Tisha looked toward the table and then back toward the kitchen, obviously not knowing what to do.

Eden jumped to her feet and laid a hand on Tisha's shoulder. "I'll go to her."

"Thank you, Eden."

Eden hurriedly made her way into the kitchen, spying the children coming in from the back yard. Randal was carrying the little one in his arms. Her knees were scraped and bleeding.

"Give her to me," she ordered and took the baby from the boy's arms. She hugged the child to her chest to calm her down. "You're going to be just fine," she reassured the child. She turned to the girl's sister. "Patsy, you and your brother go get a wet rag. Hurry."

Jack fidgeted with the back of the refrigeration unit, stopping in mid motion when he heard Eden's voice. She damned well knew English. And she spoke it better than most Americans. He peeked out from behind the unit, careful not to let Eden see him. She was kneeling on the kitchen floor hugging the baby to her breasts in a matronly fashion. The baby's tears fell onto her chest wetting the material of her dress.

What an ugly dress, he thought, until she sat the baby on the floor and straightened her back. Jack almost dropped the screwdriver he was using when he realized he could see her dark nipples through the thin, wet material.

It brought his thoughts back to her in the bathtub, and he closed his eyes and took a deep breath trying to slow down his libido. He'd been too long without a woman and he'd have to see about changing that soon. He was feeling like a teenager, unable to control his sexual urges. Still, he couldn't help himself from wondering what she'd look like in a short skirt or high heels. Anything would be more appealing than the old-lady dress she was wearing. He'd have to talk to Ruthie about this.

But for now, he'd stay quiet and just watch and listen from behind the fridge. He rather liked hearing her voice, though at the moment he could wring her neck for making him feel like a fool.

"What's the matter?" Ruthie came up behind Eden. Eden picked up the child and latched her onto one hip in a natural way.

"Nicola just got a scrape." She smiled. "She'll be fine."

"Okay," said Ruthie. "I'll let Tisha know. She's in the middle of taking an order."

Ruthie headed out the door, and Jack watched Eden bounce the little girl on her hip and make her smile. Nathan and Patsy came running back with a wet rag and

Eden took it from them and wiped the baby's elbows and knees. "Let's go back outside, shall we?"

Nathan and Patsy ran behind Eden as she made her way out the screen door and into the back yard.

Jack stood up and stepped out from behind the refrigeration unit, staring at the door as it closed behind Eden. What was this game she was playing with him? Why hadn't she told him she knew English? And why had Ruthie kept it a secret from him as well?

Ruthie walked back into the kitchen and spied Jack.

"Jack—I didn't know you were back there. How long have you—"

"Long enough to know both you and Eden lied to me. Why didn't you tell me she spoke English?"

"You never asked me." Ruthie took the empty tray from under her arm and laid it on the metal counter. "And Eden didn't lie either. I'm sure if you would have asked her if she spoke English, instead of jumping to the conclusion she couldn't, she would have told you." Alfredo was busy preparing food and stacked the full dishes under the warmer. Ruthie loaded them on the tray as she spoke.

"Well, why did she keep it from me?" he asked.

Ruthie stopped loading the plates and looked at him. "Well, why don't you ask her? Now that you know she can talk to you, this would be the perfect opportunity for you to bring up the question, don't you think? Besides, I don't want to get involved."

Suddenly Jack felt like a fool for the way he'd been talking to Eden. Not to mention embarrassed by some of the things he had said.

"Ask her?" repeated Jack. "No, I don't think so." Jack set down his tools on the counter and leaned closer so only Ruthie could hear him. "Don't mention a word to Eden that I know."

"Like I said, Jack. I don't want to get involved. But you two have got to start talking sometime. Why don't I call her in her right now?"

"Not yet, Ruthie." He grabbed two dishes of food off her tray. "Not yet."

"Hey, what are you doing? Those meals are for the customers."

"So get Alfredo to make you more. We're not that busy. And tell Eden I want to see her up in my apartment."

"What are you up to?" Ruthie cracked her gum and gave him that all-knowing look. She was worse than a mother at times, and he could just hear her already scolding him for something.

"You don't want to get involved," answered Jack and headed up the stairs with the food.

Chapter 7

Eden was a bit nervous, purposely leaving the door open when she entered the room. Ruthie hadn't told her a thing. Just that Jack wanted to see her up in the apartment. Alone. And Ruthie refused to come along with her even though Eden begged her to. Ruthie said she didn't want to get involved, but Eden knew she was just as curious about the whole matter as she was.

Her eyes scanned the large open room, but she didn't see Jack anywhere. But she saw two plates of some sort of chicken dish with golden potatoes sitting on the table. She was famished. She hadn't eaten anything since that piece of cherry pie he'd left in the room for her the night before. Her mouth watered and she took a deep breath, breathing in the delicious aroma.

"You like that?"

She hadn't heard Jack enter and turned around so quickly she became dizzy and held on to the chair for support. Jack stood in the doorway with a bottle of wine and two goblets. He had changed out of the clothes he'd been wearing earlier and now had on a tight pair of black jeans and a beige chambray shirt that was unbuttoned down to his navel.

"Just thought we'd get to know each other over a bite of lunch." He winked at her and, without turning around, used his foot to slam the door shut. He then made his way over to the table and put down the goblets and held the wine out for her to see.

"Dominique Laurent, 1995," he said. "It's one of my best wines. One hundred and twenty five dollars a bottle. I only open a bottle for special occasions."

Eden felt her lip quiver as she tried to smile.

Jack took a corkscrew out of his back pocket and stuck it into the top of the bottle. She watched his strong hands turning the corkscrew, his chest muscles flexing as he used a bit of force. She wondered what it would feel like to rub her hands over his smooth chest. Then she wondered what it would feel like if he ran his hands over hers.

The cork left the bottle with a loud pop, and Eden jumped in surprise. She had been so lost in her thoughts that the noise shattered the illusion occupying her mind.

Jack poured a glass of wine and handed it to her.

She started to reach out to take it, and then pulled back. She wasn't sure she wanted to accept anything Jack had to offer. Not when he had that sultry look on his face and she was having impure thoughts of her own.

"Go on," he coaxed. "Or are you too young for this stuff? How old are you anyway?"

She didn't like to be belittled like that. Maybe she was only twenty years of age, but in Peru it was like being forty. If only he knew she'd been drinking chica, a Peruvian beer, since she was a child. Not to mention trago, the cane liquor her mother served. These were everyday drinks back home.

She took the glass anyway and looked at it in her hand. She could smell the musty aroma of fermented grapes, and this brought memories back of the vineyards of home. She longed for the fresh air of the mountains. She longed for the open vast spaces and the blue skies with endless fluffy clouds. Everything was so different here. So closed in. So unnatural.

"Sit."

She realized Jack was holding out a chair for her to join him at the table. She felt a bit light-headed from not eating and decided to sit would be a good idea. Not that she wanted to join him—or so she tried to convince herself.

Jack took a seat across from her and held his glass up in a toast. "To life!" he said. "To finding out about ourselves and finding out about each other." He clinked her glass with his, took a sip, closing his eyes for a second as he savored the taste. He gave a small groan of approval and Eden couldn't help but notice the look of satisfaction on his face. She watched his tongue as it shot out to lick his lips, her own eyes closing as she felt a rush of heat encompass her.

He cleared his throat and her eyes shot open to meet his. Their gazes locked for a brief second then she noticed him motioning with his eyes toward her glass, willing her to join him.

"Drink," he commanded.

If for no other reason than to have somewhere else to look, she obeyed and raised the glass to her lips. It tasted good, fruity and full bodied. She'd taken a sip and was about to put it down when Jack picked up the bottle and gave her another splash before refilling his own glass.

"So. I see you got a new dress today when you went shopping." He put a piece of food in his mouth, and his eyes settled on her chest. "Nice. You could have chosen something a little younger looking—but still, I'm enjoying the view."

Eden let her eyes fall to where his were settled. To her horror, she realized her dress was wet from the baby's tears and he could see right through it. She quickly crossed her arms over her chest and lowered her head. Why was this happening to her? With the way he was looking at her, she may as well be naked.

"Don't hide," said Jack and plucked the hat from her head, throwing it on the bed behind her.

Now she really felt naked. She wanted to jump up and retrieve her hat, but to do that she'd have to lower her arms and expose herself to Jack's roving eyes.

"Why don't you eat before the food turns cold?" he said.

Eden grabbed the fork in one hand, her other arm still crossed over to her shoulder. Jack made her nervous, and when he was around she couldn't think straight. Maybe if she ate something she could rid herself of the feeling that Jack was trying to seduce her.

They ate in silence, Jack refilling her wine glass every time she took a sip. She wasn't sure how much she'd drunk, but it was relaxing her and eventually she lowered her arm from in front of her. When they were finished, Jack pulled a cigarette from the packet in his shirt pocket and stuck it in his mouth. He then patted his chest, looked around the room and stood up, shoving his hand into the tight front pocket of his jeans.

Eden's eyes followed his hand as he searched for a matchbook. His groin was eye level and she couldn't help but staring.

"Damn! Where'd I put those matches?"

Eden knew there was a book of matches lying on the bedside table and caught herself just as she was opening her mouth to tell him.

"What is it?" asked Jack. He took a step closer, his groin now directly in front of her face. "What are you looking at?"

That made her blush. She could feel the heat rise in her face. He must know she was looking at him in the same way he'd been looking at her a few minutes ago.

He removed the cigarette from his mouth and threw it on the table. "What do I have to do to get you to talk, Eden?"

She turned her head and looked out the window. She couldn't bring herself to talk now, even if she wanted to.

"I'm not used to people ignoring me when I'm talking to them."

If only he knew she wasn't ignoring him, but desperately trying to ignore the feelings she'd been having since he had entered the room.

"Do you hear me?"

She couldn't look back at him or he'd see her blushing. He'd know she was having thoughts about what lay beneath those tight black jeans.

"Look at me, Eden."

When she didn't respond, he pulled her from the chair. Immediately she cursed him out in his own language.

"Stop it," she spat. "Get your hands off me. I'm not some sort of—" she stopped in mid-sentence and covered her mouth.

"Some sort of what?" asked Jack. "You've been playing me for a fool and I don't like it. Why didn't you tell me you knew English the first day I met you?"

"I played you for a fool?" she asked. "You were the one treating me like a fool with the way you spoke to me. Not to mention telling me I looked frumpy or smelled like llama. Plus you were in such a hurry to tell everyone I did-n't know English, that you somehow forgot to ask me if it was true!"

"Eden, you can stop now."

"I'll stop when I'm good and ready to stop. You called my father a swindling souse and me a child. Who's treating whom like a fool?"

"Eden—"

If she would have slowed down, she would have realized Jack was no longer angry, but smiling.

"And then you insist I get new clothes. And you're irritating the heck out of me every time you pluck my hat from—"

Her words were cut short when Jack pulled her into his arms and kissed her. She found herself speechless as he brought his head up from the kiss.

"That's more like it," he said. "Nice and quiet."

"Quiet?" she asked and looked up into his gentle eyes. "I thought you wanted me to talk."

"So did I," he answered, looking at her mouth. "So did I."

She looked at his mouth and felt herself wanting to taste him again. She liked the way it felt to be in his arms. Safe. Caring. Exciting. And she liked the way it felt to kiss him. She daringly brought her lips to his this time and closed her eyes as his hot kiss sent her head spinning. It was either the kiss or the wine, but either way, she liked it. She put her hands around his neck and let the kiss deepen. This time Jack let his tongue trace her lips, and she opened for him the way a flower opens its petals to the sun. She never dreamed her first kiss would be so exciting. Neither did she ever think it would be with an American man.

She melded into his arms and let her hands trail down his bare chest as she leaned into him. He felt wonderful beneath her fingers. Hard muscle and sinew. Smooth, warm skin. He ran his own hands down her back and around under her arms. He was getting awfully close to her breasts, and wickedly enough she wanted him to feel her the way she'd just felt him.

Instead, he stepped back and cleared his throat. She couldn't help but feel confused and disappointed. He pulled another cigarette from the pack on the table and once again started searching his pockets. It was then she noticed he could no longer fit his hand in his front pocket, and she knew why he had turned away.

"Over by the bed," she told him.

"What?" He looked up at her in surprise and she knew what he'd had on his mind. It wasn't far from her own thoughts at the moment.

"On the table," she corrected his thoughts. "Your matches are on the bedside table."

"Oh. Yeah. Thanks." He let his gaze linger on her for a moment, and she thought he was going to come back to her for another kiss. She wanted him to. Instead, he lit the cigarette and plopped down on the bed. His shirt was totally open now as he leaned against the headboard and stretched out his legs in front of him.

He blew a puff of smoke into the air, and she watched the ringlets float to the ceiling. She'd heard about things like this. A man would take his woman and then have a smoke to try to calm down. Is this what he was doing right now? Trying to calm down? Or was he in his own way, claiming her as his woman?

"I guess I should have mentioned I knew English from the start." She walked over and sat down on the bed next to him.

He jumped up and paced the floor. "Well, I guess that would have helped, wouldn't it?"

She remained silent, not knowing what to say.

"Why didn't you?" he asked.

"Probably for the same reason you didn't tell me you'd found out."

"I was just trying to get to know you, Eden. To figure you out. To see if you were trying to swindle me like your old man did."

"He didn't swindle you!" Eden jumped to her feet.

"Like hell he didn't, sweetie. He convinced me to invest my money in something I knew nothing about. I trusted him, and he let me down. What was I supposed to think when you showed up?"

"That I was someone who needed your help?"

"That's what everyone wants from me, Eden. And they know I'll help them because I believe in people. I feel for them. I think of myself when I was younger and—oh never mind. It doesn't matter. All that matters is that I never get anything in return."

He smashed his cigarette out in an ashtray and walked over to look out the glass wall of windows that overhung the back yard. He cranked open one of them, and Eden felt the cool breeze hit her in the face. She could smell damp earth in the air.

"So, are you saying you're not going to buy me a ticket back home?" Eden slid her hat off the bed and put it on her head.

"Why should I?" Jack's arms were crossed over his chest as he stared out the window. "What's in it for me?"

Eden knew she didn't have anything to offer. She was a lost soul in a world of strangers. She'd manage to adapt to the city ways since she had spent time with her father in

Lima. Her father had made sure she'd gotten proper schooling, and that she'd seen the city and other towns as well.

"I know how you feel." She took the burlap bag out of the dresser, suddenly feeling her gift was a bit meager. She looked down to the lonely Bible in the drawer, a rush of emotions coursing through her body. She couldn't help thinking of the special times she had spent reading it with her father. It was the link that brought them together every summer. One of the most precious and valuable things she owned. This was all she had left to remember him by now. This and his photo in the locket around her neck.

She picked it up carefully and held it to her heart. Then she made her way to the window where Jack stood. "I don't have anything to offer you in return. Only this."

He turned around and raised an eyebrow, and she held out her humble offering. A bag of seeds and a Bible.

"What the hell is that, Eden? A Bible? I think it's a bit late to help me in that area. I've been pegged to go to the underworld since the day I—for a long time now."

She pulled back the Bible, a bit relieved he didn't want it. "Then how about these?" She handed him the sack of seeds. "My father told me on his death bed, this was to repay his debt."

He took the burlap bag from her hand and shook some of the contents into his palm. He then handed her the bag and stared at the beans and seeds he held.

"What is this? Some kind of bad joke?" He took the seeds and threw them out the open window. "This isn't some kind of fairy tale where I can sprout a beanstalk and find a goose that lays golden eggs. I wish it was that simple, Eden, but it's not. I'm going broke, and if I don't find a way to get money soon, I'm going to lose the restaurant."

He stormed across the room and headed for the door.

Eden felt her heart drop to her feet. The precious gift from her dying father hadn't made Jack happy. Instead, he'd treated it as meaningless and thrown some of the seeds out the window. He'd even scoffed at the idea of reading the Bible.

Eden didn't know how her father intended the gift to help Jack, but she knew her father would never lie to her. She knew somehow the seeds were the answer to Jack's prayers.

"I'm sorry," she said quietly, and Jack stopped in his tracks, his handle on the doorknob. He looked to the ground but didn't turn around.

"No, Eden. I'm the one who's sorry." And with that, he left the room.

Chapter 8

Jack spent most the rest of the day trying to avoid Eden. He didn't want to see her after the kiss they'd shared. He didn't want to feel anything for her. After all, she was the professor's daughter, he reminded himself. A daughter to the man who had taken his money and ruined his life.

If only he could pay his employees what they deserved. But now, the competition from The Ruby across the street would only make matters worse. He had to figure out a way to make money, to build back up the image of The Golden Talon before his father returned.

The door to the restaurant swung open and his competitor, Martin Noble entered with a gaudily dressed woman at his side.

"What the hell do you want?" snapped Jack as they made their way to the podium.

"Now is that any way to talk to one of your paying customers, Jack?" Martin Noble looked at the woman on his arm, and she batted her eyelashes toward Jack.

"Don't tell me you've come here to eat?"

"Well, a man gets hungry watching the progression of his own restaurant. Now are you going to give us a table or not?"

Jack was about to tell Noble where to go when Eden came down the steps, obviously having overheard every word.

"We have a nice table for two over by the window," she said and snatched up two menus as she walked up to them.

Jack could have crawled under the table at the moment. Eden had donned her native clothes again and was wearing that ugly hat. It wasn't bad enough that Jack was being humiliated by a man who would no doubt put him out of business, but now he would be the laughingstock of the neighborhood as well.

"What's this, Jack? Hiring more minorities and taking more misfits off the street again?" Noble asked.

"What's it to you, anyway?" growled Jack.

"Doesn't matter to me," answered Noble. "I just thought you'd want to know the talk on the street is that you've slandered your father's good name by taking in minorities, misfits, and probably illegal aliens as well." He looked at Eden when he said the latter.

Jack was about to start an all-out brawl with the man when Eden stepped in and took Noble's arm.

"Sí, Señor Noble, I'm not a citizen of your homeland. I'm from the mountains of Peru."

"Peru?" asked the girl on Noble's arm. "Where's that?"

"It's far from here," Eden answered. "I'm here as Jack's guest and will be leaving soon. But while I'm here, I'm helping out at the restaurant, so please follow me while I seat you."

Jack watched in awe at the way Eden handled the situation. She hadn't seemed upset at all with Noble, though Jack knew she was probably steaming inside at the way the man belittled foreigners. He walked to the busser's stand and poured himself a cup of coffee, wondering what had just happened. A man whom he despised had walked into his restaurant and insulted him and his employees, and now he was being permitted to stay and eat as well. Jack took a sip of coffee and watched as Eden made her way back to the hostess stand to seat another couple. He had to admit she was good with people. She even had Martin Noble laughing and smiling. Something Jack knew he would never do.

But still, he couldn't allow Eden to embarrass him like this. Her and her colorful rags she called clothes. And that damned tall hat that looked like it should be on Abe Lincoln or something. He'd stop this nonsense at once. He'd put her in her place and lock her upstairs in the apartment if he had to. But whatever happened, he'd make sure she was never let down into the dining room again during business hours.

Ruthie walked up to Jack, a bus boy on her heels.

"Hey, Jack. You gave Eden a job. How clever of you. Make her work to earn her way home. What a great idea. And she seems to be good with the customers. After all, we had two tables walk in since she's come down and here comes a group of businessmen. Good tippers!" She winked at Jack and turned to instruct the bus boy.

Jack watched the group of men in suits walk in, and he watched as Eden seated them too, right near the window. He noticed passersby looking in and several of them stopping in as well.

"Hey, Jack." Ruthie walked up, finishing writing an order on a notepad in her hand. "Maybe we should tell Tisha to hang around for a few more hours? After all, it looks like we may get busy, and I'm the only waitress scheduled at the moment."

"Yeah, sure." Jack was in a daze. He didn't understand this at all, but he liked the way customers were wandering in after the normal lunch hour. "And tell Alfredo he can stay on too if he wants."

"Okay, boss. Will do."

Ruthie headed off toward the kitchen, and Jack made his way over to the hostess stand. Eden had just seated a small group of women and walked back to her post, wiping her hands on her skirt.

"Jack. I'm sorry about this. I know I was out of line. I'll just go upstairs and—"

"No. Wait, Eden. I—I think I was the one who was out of line a little. I'm sorry I—"

"There's no need to apologize," she said and headed for the stairs. "You're right that I have nothing to offer. I'll just have to find another way to get that ticket."

"No, Eden. That's not what I meant." Jack followed her and put his hand on her elbow just as she started to climb the stairs. She stopped and turned her head slightly, looking at him out of the corner of her eye. "What I meant was—well, you can stay. For as long as you'd like. I want you to."

Her eyes opened wide and she looked down at his hand on her arm. He felt the connection there as well and couldn't help but remember the kiss they'd shared. He didn't want her to think he wanted her to stay just because of that. And he didn't want her to think there was any kind of commitment in what he was offering.

"You want me to stay?" She seemed surprised.

"To work. To earn your way home," he added. "You seem to be good for the restaurant, Eden. You have a way with people. I'm offering you the job of hostess. I don't have one at the moment. I can't pay you much, but I'll give you room and board during your stay. And I'll pay for anything you need in terms of clothes—uniforms and such for work."

He watched her eyes scan her own clothes and she looked at him again out of the corner of her eye.

"You're saying my clothes embarrass you, Jack? That you don't want me to be seen working in your restaurant looking like this? That I can't wear my native clothes now that I'm in the United States? That I should forget about all my customs and traditions and throw them to the wind because you think they're silly?"

"Well— " Jack didn't know how to answer. If he agreed, she'd run off in a huff and wouldn't work for him. If he denied what she said, she'd keep wearing that damned hat and strange clothes and make him the talk of the neighborhood. Damned if he did, damned if he didn't. Just like everything else in his life.

"Well, what's the answer?" she demanded. "I want to know where I stand before I accept what you've offered."

"Well, you're welcome to do as you please while you're here." He heard his own words but didn't know why he'd said them. "Just make yourself at home."

"Home? I don't think so, Jack. Chicago is nothing like home to me. But since I've no other choice at the moment, I guess I'll take you up on your offer. For now. Until I can find another way to get that ticket."

Jack nodded his head, finding himself glad she decided to stay, knowing she had no other choice. But still, they 'd come to some sort of agreement. He wasn't sure exactly what that agreement was and decided he needed a drink of something stronger than coffee to think about it.

Another couple wandered in. Jack looked at Eden. "We've got more customers. Better get to work."

She smiled. "Sure thing, boss." She greeted the couple and gathered up menus on the way to the table. Jack shook his head, not at all sure what happened.

"So, boss," came Nathan's voice from behind him, almost causing him to jump. "You hire the circus girl or what?"

"Yes, Nathan. I hired Eden. And if I hear you refer to her as a circus girl once more I'll take that Harley of yours and—"

"Point taken," said Nathan. "Have you got a minute to talk about that order I was going to place this afternoon?"

"Yeah," said Jack keeping his eyes glued to Eden. When she smiled, her whole face lit up. She glowed. She was so alive and vibrant, just like that colorful manta she wore on her back. His life had become a bit more exciting since she walked into it. And he couldn't help but want to hold her in his arms again. To feel her warm skin against his and taste her sweet lips that made him burn with desire. "We can talk," said Jack. "But first go to the bar and find me a bottle of bourbon."

Chapter 9

Eden stood at the hostess podium and watched Jack talking to Nathan in the open room that served both as his office and the pick-up area for people who wanted food on the go. Jack didn't seem to notice her, but his eyes kept darting over to the table by the front windows that seated Martin Noble and his lady friend.

She then glanced over to Martin Noble and discovered that he was doing the same thing—but sneaking peeks at Jack. This was serious competition, and she suspected that Noble had come into the restaurant for two reasons only. To irritate Jack, and to find out exactly what his competition was doing.

Eden now felt a bit bad that she had seated them instead of letting Jack throw them out. But it had looked like an all-out brawl was starting between them, and she couldn't let that happen. No, if Martin Noble was here to spy, then they'd just have to give him something to talk about.

The small rush of customers coming into the restaurant seemed to stop, so she made her way over to the office area, hoping to hear what Jack was talking about with Nathan. She saw him take a bottle of bourbon, pour himself a drink and guzzle it. He did that twice before he put the bottle down.

Eden casually pretended to be pruning dead leaves off the plants in the atrium that lay just opposite the office. She could hear Jack grumbling about the food order to Nathan, saying they'd have to cut back somehow to save money. Then Ruthie whizzed past her in a hurry, and Jack called her over.

"What'd he order?" Jack asked in a low voice, but Eden could still hear every word.

"Steak," answered Ruthie. "Why?"

"Tell him we're out," commanded Jack.

"Out? Out of Steak?" asked Ruthie. "I can't do that. Martin Noble is a big shot around these parts. I saw his picture in the entertainment section of the Tribune just last week. He writes his own column, you know."

"I didn't know."

"He's like a movie reviewer, but of the restaurant world. He critiques and evaluates the service, food, things like that."

"I get the picture, Ruthie. But I'd rather have him complain we don't have any steak than let Alfredo burn it—and you know he will. I had three complaints alone last week about the steak being overcooked. The customers like the way my father served it. They like their meat really rare. It's the sign of a good chef."

"So, I'll tell Alfredo not to burn it."

"I've tried that," said Jack. "It doesn't work."

"Well, then let Rafael cook it. He's usually pretty good."

"He's not here yet. I had him stop and pick up a few supplies before his shift."

"Well, I can't give the table next to him steak and then tell him there isn't any." Ruthie snapped her gum.

"And get rid of the gum, Ruthie. This is supposed to be a classy restaurant."

Eden noticed the look of horror on Ruthie's face at the suggestion.

"Get rid of the gum?" she asked. "Jack, you know I need it to keep me from my little problem. I haven't eaten yet today and that food is smelling really good. One taste of the lasagna and I'll be over the edge. Last time I got rid of the gum I gained thirty-five pounds in one week. You remember. And I was a bear to be around. Even you couldn't stand me and—"

"Okay, Ruthie, okay. Keep the gum, just don't snap it around Noble."

"Gotcha," said Ruthie and snapped it as she walked toward the kitchen.

Eden saw Jack pick up the bottle again and pour himself another drink. He then lit up a cigarette, all the while glancing back and forth to Noble.

"He's gonna ruin us, Nathan. I never should have let him in here. One little mistake and he'll be writing it up in his damned column. That's all I need with the way things are going around here to begin with."

Jack's eyes darted over to Noble again, and then he noticed Eden standing by the plants. Their eyes interlocked for a mere second, and Eden felt his pain, his sorrow, and the weight of the world upon his shoulders. He needed help or he was going to crack. And she knew that she was smack dab in the center of the whole thing.

She put her head down and walked past Jack, through the bar area and into the kitchen. She'd just have to do something to help him. She'd have to make sure everything went well for Martin Noble so he wouldn't have anything bad to write about The Golden Talon.

"Alfredo," she called, getting the Mexican's attention. He looked up and smiled at her as he flipped the steaks on the grill.

"Buenos días," he called. "Is there something I can get for you?"

"Buenos días," she answered back politely. "Are you cooking those steaks for table number five by any chance?"

"Sí."

"How do they want them done?"

"Both medium rare."

Eden looked at the steaks which Alfredo was making no attempt to remove. They were a combination of still mooing to bloody with just a hint of brown. She remembered Jack's own words of how his father used to serve them. This seemed just about perfect according to that, though to her it seemed disgusting.

"Take them off, will you?"

Alfredo looked at her and then back to the steaks. "I don't think they're ready yet."

"Will you do it for me? Please?" Eden batted her eyelashes the way she saw Noble's girl doing to Jack. It worked. Alfredo scooped them up and slipped them onto plates, placing them under the warmer.

"Anything for you, señorita."

"Gracias, Alfredo."

She spotted Tisha making up a few salads at the salad bar. The woman was rubbing her large stomach, and Eden knew the baby was getting heavy for her. She needed to rest and get off her feet.

"Are those for Noble's table?" Eden asked.

"They are." Tisha rubbed her stomach again. "I'm helping Ruthie before I go. We weren't expecting this small rush."

Just then the back screen door burst open and Tisha's three kids ran in. Randal was holding a scraggly, skinny black-and-white cat in his arms and little Patsy was jumping up and down trying to see it. Nicola toddled in right behind them.

"Kitty," Nicola cried to her mother and pointed at her big brother.

"Where'd you get that dirty thing?" snapped Tisha.

"It's homeless," whined Randal. "We found it living under the shed. Can we keep it, mom? Can we, can we?"

Three pairs of sad but eager eyes looked up at Tisha waiting for her answer. Eden's heart went out to the children. They reminded her of her own half brother and sisters back in Peru. Her mother had married a Peruvian, many years after Eden was born. And Eden was happy to have a stepfather, but always longed to be with her real father.

She missed the way her baby sister, little Pia, would ride on her back wrapped up in her manta. The baby would always pull on her braid, and Eden would scold her, and she would laugh. She envisioned her brother Cirilo and her sister Isidora chasing each other in a game of tag as they ran in between the alpacas and interrupted the women weaving.

She felt lonely inside and knew Tisha's children needed their mother to be with them, since they didn't have a father to care for them right now.

"Go to your children where you belong," said Eden. "I'll make the salads and help Ruthie with the tables."

Tisha looked relieved, and her smile told Eden that the offer was truly appreciated.

"Are you sure?" asked Tisha.

"I'm sure. You go on home and put your feet up."

"I'm not puttin' my feet up till I give that dang cat a flea bath."

"Then we can keep him, mama?" asked Randal.

Tisha sighed and shook her head. "Well, I don't know how we're gonna feed another mouth—but I guess we can keep it."

"Yea!" shouted Patsy and her little sister imitated her.

"You just bring that cat back here every day," said Eden. "We can feed it scraps from the kitchen."

Tisha smiled. "Thank you."

What are you going to name it?" Eden asked the kids, bending over to get a better look at it.

"How 'bout Eden?" asked Patsy.

"Eden," repeated Nicola.

Eden laughed. "Oh, no. I think one Eden is all Jack can handle around here. Maybe you should name it something else."

"Like what?" asked Randal.

"How about Gaspar?" asked Eden. "That's the Spanish name that means treasure. And it seems to me you've got a little treasure here."

"I like it," said Randal. "We'll call him Gaspar."

"Gaspar," repeated the little one.

"Come on, kids. Let's get that kitty home," said Tisha, removing her apron.

Eden watched the small family exit the back door and wave good-bye. She was happy for them and glad to help out.

Eden took the small salads and set them on a serving tray. As she headed for the door, she changed her mind and turned back to the salad counter. Eyes narrowed in concentration, she added mixed greens to Tisha's servings. "That's better," she muttered. "And now, a little pizzazz." Quickly, she shaped a radish into a rose, a carrot into a bird with a feathery tail fashioned from the scrapings, took sprigs of curly parsley, and added the colorful garnish to the salads. "Much better!"

On her way to the dining room, she passed the bar which was void of a bartender. She looked around and saw Jack was busy still talking with Nathan, so she slipped behind the counter and eyed the bottles of wine.

"Ah ha!" She grabbed a bottle off the rack, and two long stemmed glasses, and added them to her tray. "Just what we need."

She put a smile on her face and headed for Noble's table.

"What the hell's she doing?" Jack cut off Nathan in mid-speech when he caught sight of Eden, tray in hand, heading straight for Noble's table. "I told her she was a hostess, not a waitress."

Nathan joined Jack to see what he was talking about. "Aw, let her try, Jack. The poor girl's got nothing to do."

"Nothing to do but cause trouble. And that's just what's going to happen if she's serving Noble."

Jack made his way quickly out of the office area. There was no way he could stop Eden unless he ran like crazy across the floor. Not likely, without Noble seeing him.

"Damn!" he spat and made fists at his side. This girl was nothing but trouble from day one. She couldn't follow simple orders without screwing up. He'd told her to seat customers. Period. What gave her the right to think she had the skills to wait on tables, especially Noble's?

Jack stopped at the top of the few steps that led down to the section where Noble was seated. He saw Eden taking salads—huge salads with fancy garnishes off the tray and giving them to Noble and his guest.

"Who the hell made those?" he mumbled under his breath.

Then he realized she was setting down two wine goblets and handing Noble a bottle of wine. Jack didn't need to be any closer to know she was giving Noble, his enemy, his last bottle of Dominique Laurent. The exact kind he'd served Eden. The wine that cost one hundred and twenty-five dollars a bottle. He cursed himself for telling her about it in the first place. He'd have to be careful what he told her from now on.

Jack rushed forward and grabbed Eden's wrist as she handed over the bottle.

"What do you think you're doing?" he asked her under his breath.

"Serving wine," she answered simply.

"Mr. Talon." The woman with Noble beamed. "Thank you so much for sending over your best bottle of wine. Eden told us you would have it no other way. What a way to welcome us to the neighborhood."

"Yeah, Talon," added Noble. "I was a bit surprised myself. Especially since you were ready to throw me out on my ass a few minutes ago. Maybe you got a bit of class after all."

Suddenly Jack felt very foolish trying to stop Eden from serving the wine. He'd gotten a bit of approval from Noble and to take the wine back now would only give him ammunition for his column in the paper.

He gently took the bottle from Eden's hand and placed it on the table. He pulled out his pocket knife and watched the expressions of all three as he slowly flipped it open.

"You forgot the corkscrew," he said nonchalantly to Eden. He popped up a corkscrew from his knife and proceeded to open the bottle. He then put the knife away and poured a little into a glass. He handed it to Noble to taste.

The woman giggled as Noble first sniffed it, then swirled it around in the bottom of the goblet before bringing it to his mouth.

"I guess this'll do," Noble offered. But Jack could see in his eyes that the man was impressed. He proceeded to serve the wine to his guests.

"Why are you out here, Eden?" he asked as she watched him. "I thought Tisha was making the salads."

"I made them," she answered. "I sent Tisha home."

"What!" Jack stood upright so quickly he nearly lost his grip on the bottle.

"She looked like she was having labor pains," explained Eden. "And then when her kids ran in the kitchen covered with mud and dragging along that skinny old cat, I—"

"That'll be all for now, Eden," Jack cut her off.

"A cat?" asked Noble. "In the kitchen, Jack? And what's this about someone birthing a baby and filthy dirty kids?"

"Enjoy your wine," was all Jack said before taking Eden by the arm and dragging her away from the table.

"Jack, slow down," said Eden. "Where are we going in such a hurry?"

"You're going upstairs and I'm locking you in the room before you cause any more trouble."

"Trouble?" She truly didn't understand. "What did I do wrong? Martin Noble seemed to like the wine and salads. And I'm sure he'll like his steak as well."

"Jack!" Ruthie walked by with a tray of food. It actually looked good. The steaks were done just the way his father liked to serve them. Red and runny. "Problem in the kitchen."

"It'll have to wait," he snapped. "I'm busy."

"I think you'd better hurry." Ruthie cracked her gum and motioned with her head toward the kitchen door. "Alfredo burned a dinner and there's a small fire in there. He wants to know where you keep the fire extinguisher."

"Hell and damnation, what next?" Jack let go of Eden's arm. "Get upstairs and stay there until I tell you otherwise." He took off at a half-run for the kitchen.

"Did he just order to you to go upstairs and stay there?" Ruthie balanced the huge tray on her shoulder as she spoke.

"That's what it sounds like," answered Eden.

"What's going on?"

Eden took a deep breath and let out a sigh. "I just don't understand that man at all."

She left Ruthie, but instead of heading upstairs, she went out the front door into the busy city streets of Chicago.

Chapter 10

Jack extinguished the small fire and headed out the kitchen door only to bump into Martin Noble, obviously snooping around.

"Something I can get you?" asked Jack. He hid the fire extinguisher behind his back. Of all the rotten luck, Noble would find out about this.

"Have a little fire, Jack?"

"Nothing I couldn't handle. Just a burnt dinner, nothing more."

Noble strained his neck to see through the door into the kitchen. Alfredo and Rafael were cleaning up the mess, with Eddie the dishwasher helping them. The Mexicans were explaining to Eddie what happened, and Eddie was talking back with his hands. Eddie was deaf, but still they seemed to communicate all right.

"Maybe you should get some better help," said Noble. "It seems like you've got a circus going on around here. I don't see any of the crew your father had working here before he left over a year ago."

Well, Noble knew more about The Golden Talon than Jack thought. It was true he had let his father's team go and hired people who he believed, really needed the job. The people Jack hired were all misfits in a sense, but still they were real people with real problems of their own. Just like him. And they deserved the chance to earn an honest living just as much as anyone.

"I made a few changes around here," Jack explained. "My father left the restaurant in my care, and I do what I think is best for the establishment."

"Really?" Noble chuckled. "Well, I'm glad to hear that, though I can't say you're doing what's best for business. You're not a businessman, Jack, and you know it. You should have gone back to school instead of trying to make it in the real world."

"Noble, what I do is none of your concern." Jack was furious and about ready to punch the man out on the spot, but tried to be calm, and handle things with finesse the way Eden had. "Now, if you'd please go back to your table, customers are not allowed in the service areas."

"We were just leaving. I'm waiting for Missy to finish up in the little girl's room."

"Well, please wait for her by the front door."

"With pleasure." Noble took one last glance through the kitchen door window and headed out. Jack put down the fire extinguisher and followed the man just to make sure he left.

Noble's friend Missy came out of the washroom and said good-bye to Ruthie who was just finishing ringing up their bill on the register.

"Oh, Jack." Noble snapped his fingers and turned around. "I forgot to tell you. The Ruby will be having its grand opening next weekend. You and of course your little entourage here are invited. I thought maybe you'd like to come see how a five star restaurant is supposed to be run."

"I've no intention of wasting my time in your place, Noble. I've got better things to do."

Noble made a deliberate gesture of looking the place over from ceiling to floor. "Yes, I'd say you do." He held out his arm for his companion. "Come on, Missy. It's time to go."

"Wait, sugarplums. I want to say good-bye to that charming girl from—where was it she came from?" asked the blonde.

"Peru," said Jack. "And she's not here, but I'll tell her you send your best."

"Thanks, Jacky." She batted her eyelashes again and headed out the door with a sway of her hips as she held on to Noble's arm.

"Well, how do you like that!" Ruthie watched them go and snapped her gum.

"I don't," answered Jack. "And if Eden hadn't seated them, I would have thrown them out on their ass. Noble saw enough today to write up a bad review of The Golden Talon in tomorrow's paper."

"Eden looked a bit upset after you dragged her away from there."

"I'd better go talk to her." Jack headed for the stairs, but Ruthie stopped him.

"Oh, I don't think she's up there, Jack."

"What d'ya mean? I told her to go upstairs and wait for me."

"I guess she didn't like being sent to her room. I saw her heading out the front door right after you went to the kitchen to put out the fire."

"And you didn't stop her?"

"She's a big girl. If she wants to go for a walk, it's none of my business. Besides. I don't want to get involved."

"Go for a walk?" asked Jack. "She doesn't know her way around. And if she's lucky enough to find her way back, she'll probably get mugged. It's getting dark."

Jack zipped into the office and grabbed his jacket from the hook on the wall. He slipped it on and fished the car keys from his pocket.

"Where are ya going?" asked Ruthie.

"I'm going to find Eden." Jack headed for the kitchen exit. "And when I find her, she'll have hell to pay!"

Chapter II

Eden was lost. She had no idea how to get back to the restaurant, and every time she tried to ask someone they ignored her and looked the other way. Chicago wasn't a very friendly city. Nothing like Cuzco, where everyone was nice. But then again, they may have seemed friendly because she was from their surroundings. Here she was a stranger. Here she was an outcast.

When she'd started out, it was midday. In the light it was easy to find her way around. She'd found some money lying on the ground and used it to hop aboard a bus that took her to the beach. She'd walked along the shore of Lake Michigan and watched the bikers, skateboarders, and crazy sunbathers who sat on the beach in swimsuits though it was too cold to bare that much skin. She'd felt more at home by the water. The fresh air hit her face and she'd even unbraided her hair to let the wind blow through it.

She'd gotten many looks from Chicagoens about her outfit. But then again, she'd done some looking herself at people with green hair, spiked hair, pierced body parts, and outfits even stranger than hers. She couldn't get used to all the traffic and decided to go back to the restaurant. When she'd hopped on another bus, the bus driver asked for her fare. She'd purposely spoken in the Quechua language telling him she didn't have any more money. When the people behind her started complaining they were in a hurry, the bus driver waved her on, obviously not wanting to bother with someone like her. She had taken her seat on the bus next to a sleeping old man and had watched from the window as the bus rounded corners, amazed at the amount of people, stores, restaurants, taxis, and tall buildings.

She decided Chicago was a lot like Lima, though Lima never seemed so big or crowded. And she was surprised so many people roamed the streets after dark. There were no soldiers standing on the corners with machine guns in hand like back home. And she doubted Chicago had anything like marshal law. If one went out after eleven p.m. in a group of more than two—one was shot. Simple as that.

Here, she'd seen groups of tough-looking kids around every corner. Maybe they needed marshal law here, she thought.

The bus didn't go back to the restaurant, and Eden was getting a bit concerned. It came to its last stop, and the driver told Eden she had to leave. There were two other women on the bus who exited also. They were dressed in high heels, very short skirts, and very low-cut tops.

Eden was going to tell the driver she was lost, but decided not to. If he knew she spoke English he was sure to charge her for the ride, and there was no way she could pay him.

So instead she climbed down from the bus and stood on the curb, listening to the doors swish closed behind her. It took off in a rumble and a cloud of exhaust. Eden looked around and wondered how far she was from the restaurant. Nothing seemed familiar.

"Hey, who are you?" asked one of the girls from the bus.

"Yeah," said the other. "Dominick didn't tell us he was sending another girl to work the streets. This is our corner, so get lost."

"I am lost," she said. "I was hoping you could help me find my way back."

"Back?" asked the red-head. To where? The way you're dressed I couldn't even imagine where to send you."

"I'm from Peru." Eden smiled. "But while I'm here, I'm staying with a friend of my father's."

"Yeah, well, we can't help you," snapped the blonde. "We're working."

Eden didn't need to ask what they did. At that moment a car pulled up and a man stuck out his head. The blonde ran over and leaned in the window to talk to the driver. She gave him a good view of her cleavage, as well as a good view to anyone on the street of what was beneath her skirt—nothing.

"You're never going to pick up a guy dressed like that," said the red-head. You've got to take off some more clothes and get rid of that ugly hat."

The comment about the hat reminded her of Jack. How she wished right now she was back at his apartment with him yelling at her. She longed for him to rip off her hat the way he always did. It was beginning to be a comforting thought.

Eden walked over to an empty doorstep and sat down in the dark wondering what to do. The blonde jumped in the car with the customer and zipped away. The red-head leaned against the lamp post.

Eden heard a car horn and the sound of tires squealing to a stop on the pavement. She caught sight of a little blue convertible skidding to a halt in front of the red-head.

"Trixie—you seen a girl with black braids down to her waist, wearing sandals, colorful clothes, and a ridiculous tall white hat?"

Eden couldn't mistake that voice. It was Jack. She jumped to her feet and would have run to him, but the sight of the red-head leaning over the car to talk to Jack stopped her. He'd called her by name. Obviously he was one of Trixie's customers. Eden didn't like the idea of him bedding the woman. Not after she'd been in his arms and he'd kissed her like he had.

She then remembered how he'd treated her. Like a child. Sending her to her room, and not even thanking her for trying to help out. She turned and started to walk down the sidewalk the opposite way. She was better off on the streets than with him if he wasn't going to treat her better. She wouldn't run back to him like a little lost girl. She'd find her way around. She'd make friends and survive somehow in this foreign land.

She heard the car's motor as he came down the street after her.

"Eden!" he called, but she refused to look at him.

"Eden, don't make me come out there after you. Hop in the car now before you get into trouble."

"I'm nothing but trouble, Jack. Haven't you figured that out by now?" She kept walking, and Jack drove slowly to keep pace with her.

"I didn't mean that, Eden. Hell, I don't know what I meant. Just get in the car and we'll get some dinner and talk this whole thing over."

"I don't want to talk. I just want to go home."

"So jump in and I'll take you home."

"Not your home—mine." She stopped in her tracks and looked at him.

"Is that really what you want?" he asked.

"Well, I don't want to stay around here anymore. There's no place for me. I don't fit in and there's nothing for me to do. At least nothing I won't mess up, anyway."

"Get in and we'll talk about it, I promise."

"It won't do any good."

Eden saw Jack's eyes open wide as he looked down the street. Then she heard him curse and he jabbed the car into park. The convertible top was down as always, and he jumped over the unopened door, leaving the motor running, and ran over to Eden. Before she could protest, he'd scooped her up and thrown her over his shoulder.

"Put me down right now!" Eden held onto her hat before she lost it.

"Work with me here," she heard Jack grumble. "Or neither of us will make it back to the restaurant in any shape to talk."

He dumped her into the back seat, and hopped over the closed door, quickly jamming the car into reverse. Eden started to sit up but fell backwards when he squealed his tires into a U-turn and headed in the opposite direction. When she emerged from the back seat with hat in hand, she realized a large group of teens with bats and what looked liked broken bottles were running after them. The lamplight glimmered off something shiny in the leader's hand.

"Who are they?" she asked, climbing over the front seat as they drove.

"Just the fiercest gang in Chicago," he answered, looking into his rear-view mirror. "They don't like outsiders on their turf."

"Was that a gun ?"

"It wasn't a badge of honor!"

Eden slipped over the front seat, buckling in beside him, and let out a deep breath. If it wasn't for Jack she would have been in trouble over her head. He'd come to her rescue in the nick of time. Maybe she couldn't survive out here alone after all. This wasn't the mountains of Peru, this was the inner city jungle. She didn't belong here, and she knew she'd never fit in.

"Thank you for coming to get me," she said in a low voice.

"Thanks for your help with Noble this afternoon."

She couldn't believe what he was saying.

"You mean that?" she asked, pulling her hat onto her head.

With tongue in cheek, Jack kept his eyes on the road and nodded, but didn't say anything more.

"Was he pleased with the service?" She tried to sound optimistic.

"We'll find out in tomorrow's paper, won't we?"

Eden felt a knot in her stomach. She didn't want to see that review because somehow she knew it wasn't going to be good. And appearances were everything to Jack. After all, he hadn't had a hair out of place since the day she met him. Even his clothes were always neat and clean. He'd changed them at least twice a day.

They rode in silence the rest of the way. Jack pulled into the garage and Eden followed him out into the yard. She then noticed, for the first time, stairs and a door on the outside of the garage, leading to a second level.

"What's up there?" she asked.

"It's just a room," he answered.

"Does someone live there?"

"As of tonight it'll have an occupant."

When he offered no other information, Eden decided to drop the subject.

"This yard is so barren," she said. "Why don't you plant some flowers or a garden?"

"Who has time for that?" he asked. "Besides, no one's interested in a bunch of flowers."

She was, but heck if he'd ever know. She was dying to plant and terrace the land like she did back home. It was such a shame to let the good soil go to waste.

"How bout some dinner?" Jack held the kitchen screen door open for her.

Eden entered the room and realized it smelled like left-over smoke from a fire. Alfredo was already gone, and Eddie was mopping the floor. She didn't see Ruthie or Nathan anywhere and decided she didn't want to be alone with Jack just now.

"I'll just grab some bread from the drawer." Eden walked out of the kitchen into the waitress area. Jack followed. She snatched a roll from the bread drawer, keeping her back to Jack.

"Eden, we really need to talk."

"About what?"

"About us." Jack came up behind her and gently lifted her hat from her head and put it down on the counter. He ran a hand through her long, black, windblown hair, then wrapped his arms around her and held onto her stomach.

"Us?" she asked and licked her dry lips, hoping Jack didn't notice.

He nuzzled his mouth next to her ear and she could smell his aftershave and feel the slight scratchiness of his whiskers already growing in since morning.

"I like your hair loose," he whispered into her ear. "I like you, Eden. I'm sorry if I upset you."

She licked her lips again and turned in his arms. Probably not the right thing to do because now her face was right next to his chest. The open shirt and gold chain that hung around his neck were staring her in the face. He put a gentle finger under her chin and tilted her face up to his. She lowered her eyes and wondered if he was going to kiss her.

"I was worried about you, sweetie. Don't ever do that again." He talked in a soft, soothing voice instead of being angry. She believed him.

She swallowed deeply and looked at his mouth. That must have been all the cue he needed, for he leaned forward and pressed his lips gently to hers.

"You taste wonderful," he whispered and kissed her again, but this time a little deeper. She felt herself weakening in his arms. Her fingers opened, dropping the bread to the floor. She didn't care about food right now. Jack's kisses sated her hunger. She put her arms around his neck and pulled him closer. Their tongues got acquainted, and Eden's heart beat faster. She liked Jack, even though he was so wrapped up in his problems and the world of money. Even if he didn't know where to look for happiness, maybe she could show him.

Jack's hands slid up her sides and stopped directly over her breasts. As they kissed, he fondled her, and she felt a stirring within her center. She pulled away, her eyes closed, and tried to catch her breath. Everything was happening so fast, and she didn't have time to talk herself out of this situation. Next thing she knew, Jack was nuzzling his face into her chest and nipping playfully through her clothes at her nipples.

She had never wanted a man more than she did right now. She was ready to know how it felt to be with a man. Ready . . . and curious.

He pushed up her skirt and was running his hands over her bare thighs when she heard a noise and realized Eddie, the deaf mute, was standing in the doorway trying to get their attention. Eden jumped away and smoothed down her skirt, so embarrassed that she was sure her face was beet red.

"What is it, Eddie?" asked Jack.

Eddie used his hands to convey a message, watching Jack's lips for the answer.

"Yes, that's fine. We'll see you in the morning."

Eddie left through the kitchen, and Eden found herself unable to move.

"Now where were we?" Jack started to put his arms back around her, but Eden slipped away, grabbing her hat and heading through the dining room to the stairs that led to Jack's apartment.

"I'm a bit tired," she apologized. "I'll see you in the morning."

She ran up the stairs, hoping Jack wasn't going to follow. She wasn't sure what had just happened, but it frightened her to like it so much. Jack frightened her in an exciting sort of way. She'd never known a man like him and wondered what he wanted from her.

She remembered that he had called Trixie by name. Was he a regular on the strip? Just how many women had he had? She was confused, unsure of his motives. And though she had been enjoying it, she refused to be just another of his follies.

She opened the door to the room and closed it quickly behind her. With her back to the door she tried to catch her breath. Her head was spinning from her experience with Jack. Should she have stopped him? She was a stranger in this land and starting to be a stranger to herself as well. She'd known Jack only for a few days, yet she'd kissed him. Something she'd never done with any of the men back home. And she'd let him fondle her, and she probably would have gone further if Eddie hadn't interrupted.

She locked the door and threw her hat down on the bed. She felt dirty from the streets and had sand between her toes from the beach. Maybe a nice bath would help clear her head. And a good night's rest was definitely in order.

Jack tried the handle on the door to the apartment, but to his surprise Eden had locked him out of his own home. He didn't understand the girl. She seemed to be enjoying the kiss as much as he was, yet she ran off like a scared cat.

He'd already decided he'd sleep in the room above the garage but wanted to get a change of clothes and his shaver for the morning. He was about to knock on the door when he heard the bath water running.

He couldn't help but picture Eden's naked body as she stood up in the tub and gave him a picture perfect view that first night. He was already aroused from the kiss, and this thought didn't make matters any better. He looked down and noticed the strain on his zipper.

He raked a hand through his hair, which needed a cutting, and pulled a cigarette from his shirt pocket. He lit it and took a deep drag, wondering what to do about her. She wanted to go home. She'd told him, yet deep inside he wanted her to stay. He was growing fond of her and was even forgetting she was the professor's daughter.

He'd never met anyone quite like her. She was real. Natural. Not at all like his last girlfriend, Ginny. Eden had so much more to offer.

That thought surprised him, and he found himself questioning his old way of thinking. Maybe Eden wasn't that much trouble after all. Maybe he should spend a little more time with her and get to know her.

He flipped off the hall light and let the glow of his cigarette light the way as he headed downstairs and closed down the restaurant for the night. It was so quiet when it was empty that it haunted him. Nothing like the days when his father was here and the place was buzzing with activity until the wee hours of the morning.

Now the place closed at ten o'clock. No one usually came in after nine anyway. But somehow things were going to change, he was sure of it. His life had already changed so much since Eden was left in his care. He headed out to the garage, eyes to the ground, and in the moonlight he saw the seeds he'd tossed from the apartment window.

They had fallen on the rocky slabs of broken stone that once made up a little patio. He kicked them into the dirt and stepped on them, driving them into the soft soil.

"You crazy old man," he mumbled, thinking of the professor. "How are seeds going to pay my debts?" He made his way to the room above the garage thinking that Eden was just as crazy as her father.

Chapter 12

Jack went up to the studio apartment above the garage, feeling the first sprinkle of rain on his face. He pulled out his key ring and fumbled in the dark, hoping he still had the key to his old apartment. He found it and let himself in just as the sky opened and created a downpour.

The room didn't have electricity, and it took his eyes a moment to get accustomed to the dark. The room brought back memories. Memories of his high school days and the times he'd spent partying, playing his guitar, and ditching school. He closed the door behind him, kicked off his boots and made his way to the fireplace on the far wall. There were still logs and kindling on the hearth and he pulled a match from his pocket and lit the fire.

The room didn't have heat. Never did. Had he lived there long enough, his father would have eventually installed it. His father had plans for him. He wanted him to go to college to become a doctor or lawyer or something else that sounded prestigious. But Jack had other plans. He had to get out. Had to get away from his father and all his plans for his son's future. Maybe it would have been different had his mother been alive. But she died from cancer not long after he was born. Therefore, he never even had the chance for siblings. His father never remarried but stayed lonely. He would travel back and forth to Greece to spend time with his relatives, and always wanted Jack to join him.

Jack never had a desire to go abroad. And especially not with his father. Instead, he quit school and bought a motorcycle with the scant money he had managed to save. He hoped to start a band, and that was when he'd hooked up with Nathan.

Nathan was a bit older, but he had a lot of the same interests. Music, motorcycles, girls, and drugs. And the best part about it was that Nathan had money. Jack lived with him for years, but Nathan said Jack had potential to do so much more with his life. He sent Jack back home.

With nowhere else to go, Jack returned humbly to his father's doorstep. And his father had given him a second chance. He let Jack work in his restaurant, and he never pressured him to go back to school. They'd made amends, and that meant all the world to Jack. He had worked with his father for years now, trying to be the man his father wanted him to be. His father had faith in his only son and Jack wanted to make him proud.

No one else would give him the chance his father had given him. He'd built the glass room above the restaurant for Jack. He'd given him a Mercedes convertible and basically everything money could buy. But still, Jack wasn't happy. And then last year Alastair Talon decided to live abroad for a long period of time. He'd put Jack in charge of The Golden Talon. He'd told him if he liked the way Jack handled things, when he returned in a year he'd give the restaurant to him.

Jack warmed his hands by the fire and noticed his lonely guitar leaning against the bedpost where he'd left it so long ago when he decided to become a businessman. He wondered if he still remembered how to play it. He was hesitant to pick it up, but a dormant longing inside forced him toward it.

He picked up the guitar, and in the dark made his way to a wooden chair—the only other piece of furniture in the room, over by the picture window. He pulled open the draperies and plopped down on the chair. Feet resting on the window sill, leaning back on two chair legs, he tuned the guitar, then started plucking a few chords. This had always been his favorite place to sit and play music when he felt troubled.

Then he noticed something that hadn't been there last time he lived in the studio. The glass-domed apartment was in full view across the yard. His apartment. The apartment that Eden was now occupying. All the lights were blazing, and even though it was raining he could see into the room perfectly. He could see the glass and rattan table and chairs, and he could see the large brass bed in front of the windows. He'd moved it there purposely, liking the way it felt, almost as if he was outside himself.

He plucked an old song from memory and couldn't help but keep his eyes fastened on the apartment. He saw Eden's hat lying on the bed, and when he looked a little closer, he realized her clothes were there too. Then the door to the bathroom opened and Eden walked out stark naked, drying her long dark hair with a towel.

She walked over to the bed, bent over and, letting her hair touch the ground, she briskly rubbed it dry. Jack about fell from his chair when he saw her bend over. She was right in front of the window and hadn't even drawn the drapes. He thanked the stars the room was visible only from the back yard and the alley. The tall trees that bordered either side of his property made a nice barrier from the rest of the city.

Still, he could see everything about Eden from the hair on her head to the hair down below. He put his chair back on all fours and stood up. He slowly put his guitar down and laid his hand against the window.

He watched her swing back up and the wrapped towel fall to the back of her, holding her hair. She turned toward him, stretching her arms above her head and yawning. This gave Jack a wide open view of her bronzed perky breasts, and he couldn't stop himself from looking. Her dusky nipples were huge and flat, probably nice and warm from her bath. And he couldn't help but wonder what would happen to them if he rubbed his hands over them right now, or perhaps his tongue.

His own thoughts were getting him aroused. Eden gave a quick glance toward the windows, then put her foot up on a chair and stretched her shapely legs. This gave him a full view of what lay between her thighs—something he hadn't seen in a long time. He took a deep breath and released it, thinking he'd been too damned long without a woman. Since he'd met Eden he was as horny as he was in his high school days.

Maybe it was time to visit his old classmate Trixie on the street corner. He'd never done it before, but the thought crossed his mind tonight. He throbbed below his belt and his head was telling him to go for the ride. His heart was saying differently. He knew Trixie could take care of his little problem in a hurry. But he also knew he didn't really want her. No, the only woman he wanted right now was Eden. And even after the kisses they'd shared, she'd locked him out of his own apartment.

He swallowed deeply as he watched her make her way back to the bed and pull down the covers. How he wished he was sleeping there tonight with her to warm his bed. Instead, he was staying in an unheated apartment with a cold bed that was lumpy, just like himself. He pulled viciously at the strings on the drapes, closing the sight of naked Eden from his mind.

She slept in the nude. She hadn't bought a nightgown like he'd told her to after all. This was going to drive him crazy. He didn't know how he was going to survive night after night watching her naked body tease him when she didn't even know she was doing it.

He looked over to the fire and realized it had gone out. The cool breeze from the rain was blowing into the room from the open flue, but he didn't care. He needed something to help him cool down at the moment. He was hotter than hell, and it was for a girl who wouldn't have him. He'd never had this problem before, as girls were always quite willing to give themselves to Jack Talon. He had the looks, not to mention money and a flashy car, and women always seemed to be attracted to that. Now, if only he could share that with the girl from Peru.

He ripped off his shirt and threw it on the chair. He struggled out of his tight pants and kicked them across the room. He then freed his straining form from his briefs and realized he couldn't go on like this much longer. He hopped under the cold sheets, hoping they would help him cool down, because he knew it was going to be one hell of a long night.

Chapter 13

Jack tried to keep busy all week, hoping it'd take his mind off Eden. He hadn't opened the drapes in his studio apartment above the garage in days now and didn't plan on doing it any time soon. It was easier that way, even though he knew all he had to do was open them and he'd get a good view of Eden's naked body.

He should have told her to close her drapes but couldn't bring himself to do it. If he had, she would know he'd been watching her. And if she knew that, she'd be so embarrassed she'd never let him near her again.

He made small talk with her when he saw her, but she was keeping mainly to her room since Noble's slandering article about The Golden Talon came out in the paper. Noble didn't say a word about the perfectly done steaks or bottle of complimentary wine, but he was sure to mention the stray cat and fire in the kitchen. And the big emphasis was on the foreign girl from Peru, who didn't know enough to bring a corkscrew to the table with the wine. He had called her the major flaw of Jack's restaurant. He'd called the employees incompetent, unlearned and fit only to work at a greasy spoon.

Eden saw the paper and had taken it personally. Jack told her not to let it bother her and tried to act nonchalant about the whole situation when it was infuriating him inside. He knew he never should have let Noble into the restaurant, and by God the man would never step foot in there again.

Jack tried to talk to Eden, but she kept the door locked most the time. She'd only opened it for him twice this week and that was because Jack told her he'd scare away the customers if he wasn't allowed to use his own shower. He'd been damned well living in the same clothes all week, and didn't know how much longer he could go on this way—or her for that matter. He'd been dressing in the small bathroom as he didn't trust himself alone in the room with Eden when all he was wearing was a towel. Every time he looked at her he couldn't help but remember her naked body stretching in front of the open windows. And one thought like that had him so aroused, a towel around his waist wouldn't keep his secret.

He walked out of the bathroom, fully dressed and heard a knock at the door. Eden was doing nothing to answer it, only staring out the window.

"It's probably Ruthie with your food," he said, putting on his watch and the gold chain around his neck.

"I'm not hungry."

Jack shook his head and went to the door. He didn't know how to pull Eden out of this depression. He had his own problems eating away at him, and he just didn't have it in him to try to solve hers as well, whatever they were.

He pulled open the door, expecting to see Ruthie but instead Missy, Noble's girlfriend, was standing there in a sexier than hell dress clinging to her curves. Her spiked,

studded heels were a bit too much for so early in the morning.

"What do you want?" asked Jack gruffly. "Noble send
you over to spy?"

"I'm here to see Eden," she said.

"Eden's not seeing anyone this morning—or at least not
you!"

"Let her in, Jack." It was the first time Eden had said
more than three words to him all week long.

Jack stepped aside and let Missy enter. He then went
over to the dresser and picked up a brush. Looking in the
mirror, he pretended to fuss with his hair, but really wanted to know why Missy came calling.

"How are you?" asked Eden.

"I'm fine," said Missy. "But since Martin's been so busy
with the restaurant, I've been a little bored. I was wondering if I could take you to brunch. I've just moved here and
don't really have any friends."

"She's not looking for friends like you." Jack looked at
Missy in the mirror when he spoke. "And neither you nor
Noble are welcome on my property again."

He could see Missy's astonished look and Eden's scowl.

"I'd love to go," said Eden. "I'm bored, too. I don't have
any friends either, so I think we'll get along just fine."

Jack put down his brush and turned to look at Eden.

"Eden, what are you saying? This is Noble's girlfriend.
Noble! The man who said all those bad things about us in
the paper."

"Noble said them, not Missy," replied Eden.

"That's right," agreed Missy. "I like Eden and your employees and you too, Jack." She winked at him.

"That's just great," mumbled Jack and turned back to the mirror.

"And I thought we could go shopping after we eat," Missy rattled on. "I need a new dress for the grand opening of The Ruby and figured you'd want to get one too."

"We won't be there," Jack interrupted. "None of my employees, nor I, nor Eden are coming."

Eden crossed her arms over her chest and raised her chin. "I would like to get something appropriate to wear for the grand opening, but I don't have any money. I'm sorry."

"No problem." Missy laughed. "I'm loaded. My daddy left me everything when he died. Heck, I'm even going to be half owner of The Ruby soon."

"You're what?" Jack turned around quickly and looked at Missy. He couldn't believe what he was hearing. Someone like Martin Noble was taking on an airhead for a partner? It was obvious he was using her, and the girl didn't have enough brains to figure it out.

"Come on, Eden. If we leave now we can make it to brunch before it gets too crowded. We've got a lot of shopping to do and don't want to waste too much time eating."

Eden picked up her manta from the bed and tied it around her shoulders. "I'm ready," she told Missy.

"Hold on!" said Jack. "You're not going anywhere."

Eden stopped in her tracks and looked at him with determination in those huge blue eyes. He knew once she'd made up her mind there was no stopping her. He knew she had every intention of going to The Ruby's grand opening, and he could do nothing to change her mind.

"Pardon me?" she asked with sarcasm in her voice.

Jack felt restless under her perusal. She was in his care, but he didn't have any control over her. She'd proved that when she took off by herself into the streets the other night. If he told her she couldn't go now, she'd probably disappear again, and he couldn't let that happen. He cared for Eden, plus he didn't have time to be running after her every night and keeping her out of trouble. She was bored. That was obvious. She'd refused to be seen downstairs since the article came out in the paper. She was driving him crazy the way she just sat in the room day after day and did nothing but stare out that damned window. Maybe a friend was what she needed right now. Maybe this little excursion was just what the doctor ordered.

"Like I said, Eden—you aren't going anywhere—without this."

He pulled his American Express card out of his wallet.

She looked at it and pulled back a little.

"Take it," he said. "Your father left you in my care, plus I told you to buy some clothes last time and you didn't."

"I bought a dress," she said.

"And you never wear it," he answered. Actually, it was so ugly he was glad she didn't wear it. Plus he knew why. He'd seen her nipples through the thin material and he knew she wouldn't don it again if her life depended on it.

"Buy as much as you like," he told her. "You deserve it, sweetie."

"I deserve it?" she asked. "For doing what? Ruining your business and your reputation?"

"That already happened long before you arrived, Eden."

"Then maybe I deserve it for something else?" She raised her eyebrows, and Jack knew she meant in payment of the kisses and fondling they had shared the other night.

"Think what you want, Eden. I only meant you deserve it for putting up with someone like me."

"What a sweetie!" cooed Missy. "I wish Martin was more like you, Jack. He makes me pay for everything and has never once bought me a present."

A present. Interesting thought. Something Jack had never thought of. Maybe he should get something for Eden, but hell if he knew what. She wasn't the kind of girl that took a fancy to baubles. She never even wore any jewelry, except for that heart-shaped locket around her neck. And even that seemed out of place on her.

Eden slowly reached out and accepted the credit card. Her eyes met his. Quickly, she lowered her head under that damned big hat of hers.

"Buy yourself something nice," he said. "And while you're at it, get yourself a nightgown."

Eden's eyes shot up, and Missy giggled.

"Oooh," said Missy. "I know a great lingerie shop just down the street. And they're having a sale on bras and panties."

Eden's face flushed and she looked away. Jack felt a bit embarrassed himself for some odd reason.

He cleared his throat. "Yeah, well. Make sure you get some of those, too."

He made a beeline for the door and left the girls standing there. He sped down the steps and into the bar area.

"What's the hurry?" asked Nathan, strolling over to join him.

Jack poured himself a shot and downed it.

"You start drinking again, Jack?" asked Nathan. "Whiskey before ten o'clock isn't usually your style. I thought you gave up that shit years ago."

"Yeah, well, that was when I was wild and carefree and didn't have these kinds of problems."

He downed another shot and watched Missy swaying her hips down the stairs, and Eden trudging along behind her.

"You mean with the restaurant," said Nathan.

"No," said Jack as Missy waved a cute good-bye and Eden refused to look at him as they headed out the door. "No, I mean with a certain stubborn woman."

"Eden?"

"Eden."

"What's she doing now?"

"She's going to The Ruby's grand opening tomorrow night."

"No kidding!" Nathan pulled out a cigarette and lit it. He then offered one to Jack, who refused. "And after you forbid any of us from going."

Jack dug in his pocket and pulled out his car keys. "Take over for me, Nathan, will ya? I'm going to be out awhile."

"Where ya goin'? We haven't even opened yet. Not to mention you look like hell."

"Yeah, well, I plan on getting a shave and a haircut. That is, right after I buy myself some new threads."

"What's the occasion?" asked Nathan. "You haven't bought much since you've been on this strict budget."

"Well this I gotta do," grumbled Jack.

After all, he couldn't look like hell when he showed up at The Ruby's grand opening.

Chapter 14

Eden hadn't seen much of Jack since early yesterday. She'd been too busy spending time with her new friend Missy. Brunch and shopping had been the most fun she'd had in a long time. Missy bought a slinky black strapless dress for the grand opening and had Eden trying on things she never would have dreamed of wearing before she'd come to the States.

Eden stood in her room, staring at herself in the dresser mirror, not sure she was doing the right thing going to The Ruby's opening after all. Jack didn't seem happy about her decision. Matter of fact, he seemed downright disturbed. And she'd caused him enough trouble already and felt bad about putting him through more stress. Still, she'd accepted the offer from Missy for two reasons. She was bored out of her mind, and she wanted to show Jack she had a mind of her own. All along, he had treated her like a child. And maybe her father left her in his care, but that didn't give Jack the right to plan her future as well.

"I don't know about this, Missy." Eden looked at herself in the mirror, now wearing the new dress Missy herself had convinced Eden to buy. "I didn't look quite so—naked when I tried it on in the store."

"You look fantastic, Eden. You'll catch the eye of every man there."

Eden swallowed deeply as she surveyed her figure in the mirror. She'd chosen a bright colored dress like her native clothes, but Missy had told her white would look stunning against her dark complexion. Eden had chosen a dress that covered most her skin, but Missy put it back on the rack and chose this for her instead. This dress was so tight and clingy, so short, and with such a plunging neckline, that Eden felt like it was her second skin.

She looked at her breasts all trussed up in the strapless miracle bra that made her look twice her size. She had so much exposed cleavage, she was afraid to bend over for fear she'd fall right out.

"Maybe I should wear my saco over this," said Eden.

"Your what?" asked Missy.

"My jacket," Eden explained and pointed to her native clothes lying on the bed.

"Don't be so timid," scolded Missy. "You have a great body and should feel no shame in letting others know it's there."

Well, there was no doubt after tonight everyone in the city of Chicago would know exactly what Eden Rameriz's body looked like. But Eden had to admit, she kind of liked the way it felt. She did have a half-way decent figure and she felt pretty, or sexy as Missy said, by wearing this dress. Missy had even introduced her to panty hose and high heels. She'd almost twisted her ankle in the heels, but Missy said she'd get used to them. They made her taller, and as Missy explained, men liked tall women. Something Eden was not.

"Don't you think I should wear panties under this?" asked Eden.

"You've got on the panty hose, Eden. You don't want to wear panties or it'll show lines under your dress."

"Is this really what all women do?"

"It's what I do." Missy smiled as she squirted Eden with some of the new perfume she'd bought as well. "Now let's get to that makeup, shall we? And then we'll do your hair."

Eden looked at Missy's face, loaded down with colors of makeup that reminded her of the paint the Amazon tribes of the jungle wore. It might be fine for Missy, but Eden wouldn't have that junk on her face. She liked a clean, fresh feeling face. The way she felt when she'd visit the ruins of the Incan empire in Machu Picchu, where she'd spent time with her father.

Being on the top of the world, one didn't need to hide their face behind makeup. The warm sun and the cool breeze in the Andes had made her skin bronzed and her cheeks like rubies. She didn't need the makeup the city girls used to make them look the same way.

"I think I'll pass on the makeup, Missy. But thank you just the same."

"Then we'll do your hair. We've got to get rid of those braids. Maybe we can put your hair up in a bun or some-thing." Against Eden's wishes, Missy started unraveling the braids and running a brush through her long, black hair. It fanned out around Eden and fell to her waist. Eden pushed it in front of her and used it to cover up her breasts.

"Eden. We really should put your hair up."

"I like it this way."

"Have it your way." Missy sighed. She looked at the clock radio near the bed, slipped her makeup back in her purse and clicked it shut. "It's time," she announced.

Eden's heart jumped into her throat when she heard Missy's words. It was time to debut her new image at The Ruby, and she was terrified. When she said she'd go, she basically did it to spite Jack. She never really thought she'd have to go through with it. Not alone. Not without Jack there as her anchor. But he'd made it quite clear how he felt about going to Martin Noble's place. He didn't like the man and Eden was sure he'd never be caught dining in his establishment.

"I'm not sure about this after all, Missy. I don't think Jack would like me to go."

"So what do you care what Jack says? You told me yourself that you were a free thinker and could do as you please."

Words were cheap when they came over a nice brunch and you were girl chatting. Now she knew she never should have spoken them, because if she went back on her word after all the trouble Missy went to, she wouldn't be a friend at all.

Eden pushed on the heels and wobbled over to the bed, having to hold on to things once or twice to keep her balance. She was reaching for her manta when Missy stopped her.

"You can't bring that, Eden. That's why we bought the purse."

Eden frowned at the tiny beaded handbag on the bed. Why carry it when you couldn't fit anything in it? What was the purpose?

"We'll forget the bag," said Eden and grabbed her hat and plopped it on her head.

Missy looked at her and started laughing. "Oh Eden, you have such a sense of humor. You wear that into The Ruby and you'll get everyone laughing."

"I feel secure wearing my montera," said Eden. "I either wear the hat or I won't go."

She was hoping—praying that Missy would tell her she couldn't come dressed like that. That she would be too embarrassed and that Eden would have to stay in her room after all. Nice and safe and without showing her cleavage or legs to the public.

"Okay." Missy giggled. "Wear the hat. It'll be fun. I can't wait to see Martin's face."

Eden felt the knot in her stomach. What ammunition for Noble's next column. And what would Jack say when he read it? He'd be furious. She had no doubt about it. Eden tossed the hat on the bed and reluctantly followed Missy out the door.

🌿

Jack paced the floor nervously, waiting for Eden and Missy to come down the stairs. They'd been up there a long time and he wondered what they were doing. He'd had time to change in the restaurant's washroom and even shaved at

the sink and trimmed a few stray hairs from the quick haircut he'd gotten while he was out yesterday picking out a
suit.

Jack felt uncomfortable in his three-piece black Armani
suit. It wasn't what he usually wore in his own restaurant,
and the few customers they had were actually staring. It
might have been like this when his father was here, but
since then Jack had made The Golden Talon a much more
casual place. He straightened his tie which threatened to
choke him and glanced at the Rolex on his wrist. The grand
opening had started an hour ago. If they took any longer,
he was going to change his mind about this whole lame
decision.

Ruthie walked up and gave a cat call. "Gee, Jack. Got a
date or what?"

"Why do you say that?" Jack was a bit jumpy. He did-
n't really want the employees to know where he was going
and was hoping to sneak out before anyone noticed him
standing there at the bottom of the steps.

"Well, let's see." Ruthie cracked her gum. "Jack dresses
up in a three-piece suit, gets a haircut and shaves, not to
mention smells like the cologne department at Saks Fifth
Avenue."

"I just felt like dressing up," answered Jack nonchalantly. "And can't a man get a haircut or put on some aftershave without everyone getting suspicious?"

"And I suppose the corsage is for your lapel? Just for the
heck of it?"

Jack looked down and realized he was gripping the flowers so tight he was nearly crushing them. He'd chosen a beautiful huge purple orchid with a small spattering of white baby's breath for Eden. He wanted to somehow make amends for the way he'd been acting and was hoping this would do the trick.

"Oh all right, Ruthie. If it'll stop you from breathing fire, I'll tell you. I'm going over to The Ruby's grand opening."

"You're going to The Ruby?" Ruthie's voice was a bit loud, and Tisha walked over with her kids, having just finished her shift.

"You're going where?" asked Tisha.

"Jack looks pretty," said little Patsy, tugging on his pant leg. "Can I smell the flower?"

Jack was about to blow his cool. He just should have let Eden go by herself and stuck to his guns about this. Martin Noble was his competition not to mention his enemy. The Ruby was the last place in the world he wanted to be tonight.

"Hey, Jack. You clean up pretty nice," said Nathan, joining the little party. Alfredo was on his heels, wiping his hands in a towel.

"Señor Jack, Did I hear we're going to The Ruby tonight for the grand opening?"

"I'm going," snapped Jack. Not you or any of my employees. We've got a restaurant to run here, so all of you get back to work and don't worry about what the hell I'm going to be doing tonight."

"Hey!" snapped Ruthie. "Watch that language around the kids."

Jack looked down at Patsy who was still pulling on his leg. The baby was sitting on the floor repeating the word hell. Randal was holding onto something which Jack realized was that stray cat they'd brought in, only now it was really fat. He could only guess where it had been eating.

"C'mon, kids, we gotta be going home now." Tisha picked up the baby and pulled Patsy off his leg. "Have a fun time at the opening, Jack. And bring us a doggy bag, will ya? We'd love to taste the fancy food Martin Noble will be serving tonight."

"Yeah, right." Jack gave one final warning and the rest of his employees, except Ruthie, scurried back to work.

"It's for Eden, isn't it?"

Jack looked down at the corsage and realized he'd crushed the baby's breath.

"Yeah."

"You really like her, don't you?"

"I'm just going to keep an eye on her so she doesn't do anything stupid, that's all."

"Right." Ruthie snapped her gum and headed off for the kitchen.

The door at the top of the stairs banged and Jack looked up to see Missy strutting down the stairs in a sexy black dress. Then he realized Eden was following her. Or at least he thought it was Eden but he wasn't all that sure.

"Hi, Jack. Don't you look spiffy!" Missy came to his side, and it was then that Jack got a good view of Eden wobbling down the stairs in a pair of high heels. Her heel caught on the bottom step and she stumbled forward. Jack grabbed for her and kept her from hitting the ground.

"What the hell do you think you're doing in those?" he asked. "Now go take them off before you break your damned neck."

Eden looked up and pushed the hair from her face. That was when Jack noticed the slinky white dress that clung to her every curve, and the plunging neckline that showed more cleavage than was morally decent. Between her breasts snuggled the heart-shaped locket, now on a gold chain.

"Eden. You look—" He didn't know how to finish the sentence. She looked sexier than all hell, and if it was possible, it was getting him more aroused than seeing her naked. "You look—"

"Beautiful!" Missy finished the sentence for him.

Jack was too dumbfounded and just nodded his head.

Eden looked him over just like he was looking at her.

"And you look as if you're going somewhere," answered Eden calmly.

"Coming with us to The Ruby?" asked Missy.

Eden's eyes widened. "Are you?"

"Well, I couldn't let you go alone," said Jack. "After all, you don't really know anybody, and you'd probably break your damned neck in those heels if you didn't have someone to hold on to."

If he wasn't mistaken, Eden almost looked a bit relieved. He helped her steady herself, and she took her hands off his arm.

"What's that?" she asked, looking at Jack's hand.

Jack couldn't take his eyes off her. He held out the flower. "It's for you," he said. "I thought you might like it."

Missy giggled and excused herself and headed over to flirt with Nathan by the register. Eden looked at Jack's hand with a strange expression on her face. Jack still had his eyes glued to her.

"Thank you—I think. But what is it?"

Jack looked down and realized to his horror that when he'd caught Eden from falling, he'd still had the flower in his hand. Its petals were broken and the baby's breath lay at odd angles, sticking out in all directions.

"Oh, Eden. I'm sorry. It was supposed to be a corsage for you to wear."

"I'd still like to wear it, Jack. Will you pin it on me?"

He hesitated. There was no way he could pin it on her without his hands brushing up against her breasts, or putting his fingers down her cleavage. And that cleavage just kept calling to him like a siren luring him to his death, and making him wish he had a drink about now.

"Let's just forget the flower and go on over to The Ruby." Jack tossed the flower on the counter and it landed next to Nathan's hand.

"Don't stay out too late now, you two." Nathan smiled at Jack and Eden, then looked over to Missy and winked.

"Sure you don't want to come?" Missy asked Nathan.

"Naw." He looked at Jack. "Someone's got to hold down the fort."

"Then come on you two," Missy said to Jack and Eden. "We're going to have lots of fun."

Jack held his arm out for Eden, and she slipped her fingers gently around it.

"Shall we?" he asked.

She licked her lips and took a deep breath. Both of her actions alluring, though she probably had no idea what she was doing to him. Missy had said they'd have fun tonight, but Jack sincerely doubted it. Not at Noble's place at least. Being at The Ruby with Eden dressed like this was going to be anything but fun.

Chapter 15

Eden clung to Jack's arm as they crossed the street and made their way through the crowd and into the doors of The Ruby. The grand opening was such a huge success, they had people waiting outside, hoping to go in as soon as someone exited.

Eden felt ridiculous in her new outfit, and now wished she had worn her native clothes. But still, if she had, she'd have no reason to hang on to Jack's arm. The heels gave her the excuse, and she rather liked it.

"They're with me," Missy instructed the men standing at the door, keeping too many people from entering and going against the fire code.

"Yes, Ms. Noble," said one of the men. Missy giggled and explained to him that she wasn't married to Martin.

Inside, the first thing Eden noticed was the grand piano and the man in a tux playing it. Music floated through the large restaurant, and waiters with their noses in the air hurried by carrying trays high above their heads.

"Sure is busy in here," said Eden.

"Umph," grumbled Jack.

"I'm going to go find Martin," said Missy. "I've got a table by the window reserved for us. We'll join you in a minute. Just follow Charles to the table."

A host stepped forward and motioned them to follow.

"I didn't know Noble would be joining us," grumbled Jack. "Hell, I don't know why I even came."

Eden knew why he'd come. Because he didn't want her going out by herself. She knew if it wasn't for her, Jack would never set foot in the place. And in a way she felt sorry she'd caused trouble for Jack once again. But still, she just had to make him see the good side of it all.

"Come on, Jack." Eden pulled at his arm, but he refused to budge. "We can't leave now or Missy would be hurt. She went to a lot of work to get me ready to come here tonight."

Jack looked her over from head to toes. She felt a wash of heat throughout her body. Part of her wanted to take her hair and cover her half-bare breasts from his gaze, but another part of her wanted him to look and have his fill. She was starting to have feelings for Jack that she didn't quite understand. He made her feel different than any of the men had from back home. He looked at her like he wanted to eat her, when back home the men just looked at her because they wanted her to make them something to eat.

"She did a good job, Eden. You look wonderful."

Her heart beat faster and she lowered her head wishing for the security of her hat she'd left in the room. Her legs got a bit wobbly and without even moving, her ankle turned and Jack grabbed her around the waist to keep her from falling.

She looked up into his eyes, and he looked down into hers. Their faces were so close it would be so easy for him to lean over a bit more and kiss her. She wished he would. She could smell his spicy cologne and see his trimmed sideburns and his bushy brows. His eyes were hypnotizing as they drank her in, making her want to run away before she ended up doing something she shouldn't.

The host cleared his throat and Eden felt embarrassed all of a sudden, wondering if the man could read her thoughts.

"If you'll follow me," he said in a stiff but professional sounding voice.

Jack turned her around, and together they followed the host to what was probably the best table in the house. It was on the second floor of the restaurant and faced the street. It was surrounded by hanging plants, brass-trimmed rails, and gaudy art pieces on shelves and on the walls. Jack pulled out her chair and Eden sat down, letting him push her in. She was a bit awkward with the action, not able to get used to it.

"Eden," said Jack as he seated himself next to her. "You seem like you've never had a man seat you before."

"I haven't. Things are different where I come from, Jack."

"Why don't you tell me about it? I'd really like to get to know you better."

"I'd like that too."

The cocktail waitress came by with a tray of champagne. "Complimentary drinks tonight as well as the food, since you're friends of Mr. Noble's," she said.

Eden saw Jack cringe at the mention of the word friend. When the waitress left, Eden continued.

"Where I come from, we don't have a chair for the men to seat me. The women squat on the ground to eat, and the men usually sit on piles of earth."

Jack was raising the glass to his mouth and stopped in mid-motion. "I had no idea. I'm sorry."

"Why are you sorry?" asked Eden. "It's the way of the Quechua people."

"I've never been to Peru," said Jack. "But I didn't think it was that much different from here."

"It's not—in a city like Lima," explained Eden. "But I come from the outskirts of Cuzco. The rural areas. The people there are much poorer. We live in one room adobe houses with thatched roofs."

"No kidding, Eden. No wonder you seem so uncomfortable here. This is all so foreign to you."

Eden raised her glass and took a sip of the bubbly liquid. It tickled her nose and she sneezed.

"I suppose you're not used to champagne either," said Jack.

"We drink chicha, a beer made from fermented corn, or trago, which is a cane liquor. Not quite like this."

"I bet not." Jack laughed, and Eden relaxed. It was good to see him smile, good to hear the deep timbre of his laugh. He seemed so preoccupied with his problems lately that she had wondered if he could ever be happy.

"I like to see you smile," she said.

"It's something I haven't done in a long time," admitted Jack. "But when I'm with you, Eden—you make me happy."

"When I'm not making you angry," she reminded him, and they both laughed.

"I'm sorry I didn't take the time to get to know you right away." Jack finished his champagne and put the glass down. He reached across the table and put his hand over hers. She felt the warmth and the comfort in his touch. She felt the sincerity in his words. "It's just that I was very angry at your father."

"He's gone now, Jack. So let it go," she said in a soft voice.

Jack gave her hand a squeeze and looked deep into her eyes.

"It's not all that easy," he explained. "I lent your father money. Lots of it, when it wasn't mine to lend. I used your father as an opportunity to make The Golden Talon flourish. And when I found out your father had gambled and lost all the money, I was furious. He had no right to do that, Eden."

Eden felt uneasy, since she didn't like anyone speaking ill of her father. She loved him with all her heart, but she knew Jack was right.

She slipped her hand out from under Jack's and put it on her lap. "My father would never do anything to hurt anyone. Not intentionally."

"Oh yeah?" asked Jack. "Then how come he never married your mother?"

Eden's hand flew to her locket to reassure herself it was still there. He was still there. Her father's photo was in the locket along with one side that was blank. She wanted the comfort of her father at that moment, and her heart ached that he was gone.

"You don't understand, Jack."

"No, I don't. But maybe you can explain it to me."

Just then, Martin Noble walked up with Missy on his arm.

"Well, Talon, I see you couldn't stay away after all. Come to check out the competition?"

"You're no competition for me, Noble. I only came because Eden wanted to."

"Eden?" Noble looked at Eden in surprise, as if he didn't know her. "Is this that Indian girl you had visiting, Jack?"

Eden fumed at Noble's use of the word Indian. It was an insult to her people to be referred to as that. But then again, even if Noble didn't know that, she couldn't expect anything different of the man.

"She's Quechua," Jack corrected Noble. "A descendent of the Inca tribe, right Eden?"

Eden just smiled.

"Well, then I guess you've never seen restaurants and nightclubs before," said Noble. "Maybe I can show you around Chicago while you're here."

Jack looked up sharply at that comment. "I'm going to do that, Noble, so don't bother yourself with it. I've already made plans to show Eden everything she needs to see."

It was obvious Jack didn't want Noble anywhere near her, and she liked that form of possessiveness. Yet it was news to Eden that Jack was going to take her anywhere. Maybe this tinge of jealousy would work to her benefit after all.

Noble seated Missy beside Jack and put himself right next to Eden.

"While I'm from a more rural part of the country," Eden explained, "Peru does have restaurants and nightclubs, Mr. Noble. They're called peñas, and Berranco, a suburb of Lima is known for its peñas."

Missy giggled at the word, and covered her mouth. "Oh, Eden you are just too funny."

The rest of the evening went so slow, Eden just wished she could go back to Jack's apartment. The Golden Talon was visible from where they sat, and Eden couldn't help but notice Jack glancing out the window every couple minutes. She knew what he was looking for. No one had entered Jack's restaurant the entire time they'd been at The Ruby. Martin Noble was pulling the business away from Jack's place. Customers were standing in line for The Ruby, but The Golden Talon was empty.

Dinner was too rich for Eden, and she couldn't even recognize some of the foods. She tried to keep small talk going with Missy, interrupting every time Noble seemed to say something to belittle Jack.

Eden felt uncomfortable in her new attire, especially since Martin Noble kept his eyes down her cleavage most of the night. She'd taken her hair and covered up her bare skin, but Missy kept giving her dirty looks and telling her behind the menu that she should show off her womanly attributes. Jack was quiet—too quiet ever since Noble had come to the table, and that made Eden even more nervous.

Right after dessert, Eden stifled a fake yawned and tried to excuse them, saying she was tired.

"I'll hear none of that," said Noble. "I want a dance with you, little lady, before you go."

He got up and grabbed Eden's arm. He pulled her to her feet and headed her out to the dance floor, which wasn't far from their table. The orchestra was just finishing warming up, and the violins started in on a slow tune. Martin Noble pulled her close to his chest. She could smell his heavy cologne, and also the alcohol on his breath.

She looked over to Jack with a pleading in her eyes. He seemed to want to come rescue her, but Missy was taking him to the dance floor as well.

"So, isn't The Ruby something else?" Noble chuckled.

"Something else," repeated Eden.

"I'm going to put Talon out of business within the next month. Wait till his father comes home and sees what Jack's done to his place. It'll totally ruin the man. And I can't wait to see his face."

"You mean you have nothing against Jack? Just his father?" asked Eden.

"Alastair Talon stole my bride," said Noble. "Jack's mother should have been my wife, but he stole her away. But Alastair will be sorry he ever married her and had Jack. Right after he finds out Jack's ruined the family name."

"Excuse me, Mr. Noble, but I have to be leaving now."
Eden pushed away from him, but he only held her closer.

"Not yet, sweetie. I'm not done."

"Yes, you are," said Jack, stepping in. "Let Eden go,
before I make you."

"Oh, you wouldn't do something like that in such a
classy place as this, Talon. Even you aren't that stupid."
Noble nuzzled his face into Eden's neck, and she could
feel his breath between her breasts.

Before Eden knew what was happening, Jack smashed
his fist into Noble's face and she was thrown from his arms.
Noble stumbled backwards into the orchestra. Missy
screamed and ran to him.

"Come on, Eden. We're going home." Jack pulled her
along with him. Eden was stumbling down the steps in her
heels, and Jack picked her up and threw her over his shoulder.

"I knew it was a bad idea to come here," he grumbled
as he pushed his way through the crowd at the entrance
and made his way across the street.

"Put me down, Jack." In the position Eden was in, she
felt like the whole neighborhood could see up her skirt and
down her cleavage. And they probably could too.

"Not with those damned shoes on. I don't know what
the hell you thought you were proving."

Eden noticed a flash that went off from somewhere in
the crowd, but didn't think much of it. She was too busy
trying to get the hair out of her face to see where Jack was
taking her.

He pushed his way through the door of his own restaurant and turned the sign to closed.

"Jack," came Nathan's voice from somewhere Eden couldn't see.

"Close up the restaurant and send everyone home," ordered Jack.

"But it's not time, yet."

"Any customers in here?" asked Jack, making his way up the stairs.

"No."

"I rest my case. Now get going and don't let anyone bother me for the rest of the night."

"Good luck, Jack." Nathan's voice was distant when Jack kicked open the door and dropped Eden onto the bed.

He started ripping off his tie and then his jacket and vest, throwing them anywhere he happened to be pacing at the moment.

"Next time you get the crazy idea to do something just to spite me, I'm going to—" He stopped in mid-sentence and looked at her.

"I'm sorry," she said. "I know it must have been horrible for you. I hated it myself."

"Then why'd you do it, Eden? Why couldn't you just stay here like I asked you to?"

Eden kicked off the heels and scooted to the end of the bed. Her dress rode up her thighs in the process, and she caught Jack eyeing her legs.

"Turn away," she said. "Or haven't you the decency to give a girl a little privacy?"

"You can have all the privacy you want, Eden. I'm leaving."

Her heart sank. He was opening the door when she stopped him.

"I don't want you to leave, Jack," she blurted out.

He stopped but didn't turn to look at her. "What do you want?" he asked. "I can't figure you out."

"I want you to stay and talk with me. I want to get to know you."

He turned his head slightly and eyed her again. He took a deep breath and released it.

"I can't stay," he muttered, facing the door again. "If I do, I won't be able to control myself. I've only had one thing on my mind since I saw you in that damned sexy dress. If you ask me to stay, I'm going to do something I may regret in the morning."

"Close the door, Jack. Regrets are only for those who live in the past. In Peru, we live for the day."

Eden didn't think he'd stay. He stood there for a moment, then opened the door wider. But instead of leaving, he turned and looked at her once more. She saw his hesitation, and also the need in his brilliant, blue eyes.

"Are you sure, Eden? This isn't something I'm going to be able to stop once we've started."

"I want you," she said, and heard the quiver in her own voice. "I won't regret it tomorrow and neither should you."

Jack gave a silent nod, then closed and locked the door.

He removed his shirt, then walked over to the window and drew the drapes. "Did you realize I could see you naked from the apartment over the garage?"

"Really," she answered, not able to hold back a smile.

"You like to tease a man?" He unbuttoned his pants and moved toward her slowly.

"Just you." She licked her dry lips and realized she was barely breathing.

She heard his zipper go down and saw him stepping out of his pants and kicking them across the room before he dimmed the lights. Her heart beat fast as he made his way to the bed without his briefs.

Eden couldn't stop herself from looking. The man was built beautifully in every way. She watched the ripple of his chest muscles as he reached behind her and pulled her native clothes and manta from the bed and placed them on the chair.

"You excite me, sweetie, in a way I've never known. You are so primitive yet advanced so far past me that it scares me."

"You excite me as well."

He was coming closer to her and she anticipated his warm body. She wanted to be in his embrace again. She wanted to taste his lips. She wanted to feel the security of his arms around her, just like the night she'd been lost in the city.

He reached out and took her hair in his hands, running his fingers through it and placing it behind her back. Eden no longer wanted to cover up her cleavage. Instead, she let him look.

"You look good enough to eat," he said. "I feel like you're little Red Riding Hood in that dress, and I'm the big bad wolf."

"Red Riding Hood?" she asked, slightly confused.

"Bad analogy, since the dress is white," he answered with a grin. "But the big bad wolf thing still holds true."

He took her face in his hands and gently brought his lips to hers. His kiss was hot, tantalizing, a brilliant sun melting the ice. She liked the way it felt. The room was barely lit by anything but the moonlit sky that shone through the glass-domed ceiling. It was just the two of them, now. The two of them and the vast sky above them, a million stars shining down on them, even if they weren't all visible in the Chicago sky.

"I couldn't help all night but wonder what it would be like to undress you." Jack gently took her by the arms and helped her to her feet.

"You've been doing it with your eyes all night," said Eden, resting her head against his wide, sturdy chest.

Jack reached out his hands and rubbed them over her bare shoulders, and she reveled in the intimacy of the touch. He then flicked the spaghetti straps from her shoulders, and she felt the dress falling from her.

Eden stood there in her miracle bra, the dress stopping at her waist as it was too tight to fall all the way to the floor.

"I see you bought a bra," said Jack.

She felt her face flush. "I would have gotten a different one, but Missy insisted this is what all the girls wore. Eden could hear the sound of her own heart, and wondered if Jack could hear it too. She took a deep breath to try to relax, but realized it only made her chest more pronounced. Jack noticed, too.

He ran his finger gently over the curves of her breast and traced a path between them. Pulling her to him, he kissed her again. His lips were soft, his hands gentle. He was a man who knew how to caress a woman. He made no secret of his wantings, nor did she want him too. She knew what she wanted as well. Jack. She longed to open her heart to him, and hoped he would do the same for her.

She wrapped her arms around his neck and could feel his hands caressing her hips and buttocks as they kissed. He then pulled the dress from her hips and let it slide to the floor. Excitement rushed through her. She could feel her body relaxing, wanting Jack more and more.

He kissed her neck, and she threw back her head in ecstasy when he ran his warm tongue around her collar bone and daringly close to her breasts. She could feel his hard readiness pressed against her, and she knew she was ready too. Then he unclasped her bra, and it fell to the floor with a soft thud.

He stepped back and looked at her in the dim light, and her first instinct was to run and hide. But she didn't. She let him look and at the same time she looked at him.

"You look so sexy without any panties under those hose."

He looked sexy to her as well, but she couldn't find the words to tell him. Instead, she let her eyes sweep down his body, lingering a bit when she got below his hips. He made a small groan at the back of his throat and her eyes shot back up to his face.

"I think it's time," he told her, flipping back the covers, easing her gently upon the leopard skin sheets. He pulled off her hose inch by inch, and Eden felt her body growing hot with anticipation. It never felt so good to be naked. And when Jack's hot, hard body pressed up against hers, she couldn't wait to feel him inside her.

He trailed kisses down her cheek and neck and stopped only to encircle the tip of her breast. Eyes closed, she arched back, feeling each flick of his tongue all the way down to her belly.

Her breathing deepened, and she bit the side of her cheek in order not to cry out when his tongue swirled around her navel.

"It's been so long," murmured Jack. "It's been too long and this feels so damned good."

"It does," agreed Eden, pulling his head back up to her chest. She moistened her lips with her tongue and tried to catch her breath.

"Been a long time for you, too?" he asked, nibbling on her earlobe.

She didn't know how to tell him she was still a virgin. To the Quechua people, a twenty-year-old who wasn't married was unheard of. Eden was basically an outcast, though she lived and worked with the people of the village, her mother insisting she had no place else to go. But she'd brought shame to her mother as well as the village. And not one of the native men wanted a woman of mixed blood.

"Longer than you think," she answered, running her hands up and down his back, loving the feel of his taut muscles as he held himself over her, leaning on his elbows.

He then put his knee between her thighs, and she pulled her legs closer together.

"Open for me, sweetie. You seem a little shy for someone who's willing."

She opened for him but tensed when she felt him trying to enter.

"What's the matter, Eden?" he asked through heavy breathing. "You're not changing your mind, are you?"

"No," she answered quickly. "I meant it when I said I wanted you, Jack."

As Jack entered her she tensed again, from anticipation, not because it hurt. Mountain women had a high tolerance for pain as life was hard, and they were very physical. She felt him deep within her as he started to rock his hips back and forth.

"This feels so good," he whispered. "You are so tight, it's driving me mad."

Eden was just beginning to relax and welcome the vibrancy she had never known, when Jack made a noise in the back of his throat and all but collapsed on top of her. He then rolled to his side and released her.

"Wow, Eden. I haven't felt anyone so tight in a long time."

She could feel the tears forming in her eyes and tried to hold them back. She didn't show emotion. It wasn't her people's way. Still, she had such pent up feelings and was so unsure of any of them. She didn't regret lying with Jack, she just wanted it to last longer.

He looked at her when she didn't respond and pushed himself up on his elbow.

"Eden, is there something you're not telling me?

She didn't answer, just looked the other way.

"Oh, shit! Don't tell me you were a virgin!"

She flinched. So he disapproved of twenty-year-old virgins, just as her own villagers had. She'd disappointed Jack as well. She should have told him before they started so he could have changed his mind.

She tried to get up off the bed, but Jack pulled her back.

"It's true, isn't it? Eden, why didn't you tell me?"

"I wanted to," she said, biting her lip trying not to cry. "But I was afraid."

Jack could have kicked himself for what he'd done. He had not only kept Eden from her homeland, but he now took her virginity as well. She was crying, though she tried hard not to let him see it. He'd made a mistake again. Had he been thinking with his head and not his zipper, he would have realized she was fragile and not ready for this.

She said she wanted him, but now he knew it was only because she wanted to please him after causing him so much trouble. But now he'd done damage that could never be undone. And he'd been so aroused he hadn't even thought to use protection.

"I'm sorry, sweetheart." He pulled her to his chest and kissed the top of her head. "Had I known, I wouldn't have touched you."

"I'm sorry," said Eden. "I've disappointed you, just like I did my own people."

"What the hell are you talking about? You didn't disappoint me—just the opposite."

"Highland girls are married at adulthood," she explained. "It's unusual and not accepted to be as old as me and not married."

"And are the girls expected to be virgins when they marry?" he asked.

She smiled and relaxed a little as she lay back down and snuggled into his arms.

"A child must be conceived before the couple are allowed to marry. The union must be proven fruitful first."

Jack felt a rush of anxiety sweep over him. Is this why she wanted him? Was she trying to conceive, and did she have marrying on the mind? Jack wasn't ready for a commitment like that. And no one was going to rush him.

"Eden, I think that after tonight we should slow down a bit."

He felt her body tense in his arms.

"You don't want me, Jack?"

"No, no. Just the opposite. All I mean is that we should get to know each other better before we do it again."

"I agree," said Eden. "I'd like that."

He spent the night with Eden in his arms. It felt good to be near her, but he knew he couldn't spend another night here. Not without wanting her, taking her again. No, tomorrow he'd go back to the room above the garage, and they'd start all over. Tomorrow he'd get to know who Eden Ramirez from Peru really was.

Chapter 16

When Eden awoke the next morning, Jack was already gone. It wasn't like her to sleep past dawn, but since she'd been in Chicago nothing was the same. She got to her feet and looked for her clothes. The white dress was in a heap on the floor, and she couldn't help but remembering her experience last night.

Making love wasn't all a mystery to her. After all, she lived in a one-room house with her mother, her siblings, and her stepfather. And many times her uncle, his wife, and his family would stay when they were helping in the fields.

There wasn't much privacy among the Quechuas. And neither did they seem to care. She was different, as she felt shy about such things. Just one more reason for them to consider her an outcast.

Eden grabbed her unco and pulled it over her head. She stepped into her pollera, buttoned the skirt, and wrapped the hand-woven belt about her waist. She pulled her short jacket over her shoulders, feeling so covered with the saco after last night. Then she slipped into her sandals, grabbed her hat, and made her way to the mirror to comb and braid her hair.

She walked to the window as she was braiding and saw Jack standing in the yard looking at something. He looked up, and she had half a mind to step back in the hope that he hadn't seen her. She wasn't sure at all how to feel after last night.

"Come here," he said and motioned with his hand.

She wondered what he wanted, and grabbed her montera off the dresser, pulling the hat low on her head as she made her way down the stairs.

"Mornin'," Nathan greeted her from the office.

"Wenos dias," she returned the greeting in the Quechua language.

She felt his eyes on her as she made her way through the kitchen to the back door.

Ruthie stopped her before she could scurry through. "So what happened last night?"

Eden's heart skipped and she wondered just how everyone knew about her and Jack.

"Was it worth it?" Ruthie continued.

Eden's eyes opened wide. "What?"

"The opening of The Ruby." Ruthie cocked her head. "You look a bit flushed, Eden. Do you have a fever?"

"I'm fine," she muttered in relief and hurried out to the back yard.

"Look at this," Jack called out.

Eden looked down and saw what Jack was pointing at. At the edge of the patio grew knee-high plants.

"You know what this is?" he asked. He looked good in blue jeans and a t-shirt with rolled-up sleeves. The slight breeze kissed her face, and she reveled in the smell of budding life all around her. It was just about summer now in the States.

Eden took a closer look. She knew exactly what grew there. The same kind of plants they farmed back home.

"It's lima beans, and grain. Chisiya mama," she said.

"Whose mama?" asked Jack, and Eden hit him playfully on the arm.

"Chisiya mama," she repeated. "It means mother grain." It's also known to some as quinoa. It was sacred to the Incas, and has so much protein they used it instead of meat."

"Quinoa," repeated Jack. "I've heard of it. I think they sell it here in the States."

"I'm sure they do," said Eden. "But I had no idea it grew here."

"These are your seeds, Eden. The ones your father gave you. The ones I threw out the window."

"It's a good sign." Eden smiled. "You're going to prosper, Jack."

"Ha!" Jack blew out air in a disgusted way. "The only way I'll prosper is if this beanstalk grows tall enough to reach some giant's castle in the sky. Then maybe I can climb it and find a goose that lays golden eggs just like the fairy tale."

Eden wasn't sure what Jack was talking about. "Fairy tale?" she asked.

"Jack and the beanstalk?" said Jack. "Oh, never mind. Why I wanted you down here was because I wanted to know if you could plant me a garden?"

"A garden?" Eden was surprised. "Weren't you the one who said you didn't need or want one? Are we talking about vegetables or flowers?"

"Both," answered Jack. "I want to learn how you farm the land back home. I want to watch you do it."

"But this is different," she said. "I don't know if—" She saw the pleading look on his face and remembered his quest to get to know her better. Maybe by doing this, she could get closer to Jack as well. And she was just dying to work with the earth again. "All right," she said. "What do you want me to start with?"

"The seeds your father gave you. I take it they're all native seeds of your land?"

"They are." Eden smiled. "After all, where do you think Lima beans come from?"

Jack crossed his arms and nodded his head. "I've been eating Peruvian beans all these years, and I never even knew it."

"Not only that, but you probably know more words in the Quechua language than you've learned in your little Spanish lesson from Alfredo."

"Like what?" he challenged her.

"Like llama," she said.

"Llama is Quechua?" Jack asked in surprise.

Eden nodded. "As well as cóndor, puma. and pampa."

"I think I can handle this Quechua stuff," said Jack with confidence. "Pretty easy."

"Not all of it. But I can teach you if you want to learn."

Jack smiled at her, and she wanted him to touch her. She loved the way his eyes glistened and his whole face lit up when he smiled. Such a warmth about him—a warmth that melted his cold façade. Yet there was a bit of caution in his eyes and he didn't reach out for her. He seemed to be holding back, and she didn't understand why.

"So when can I start?" she asked.

"You can go out this morning to the nurseries and get what you need," he said. "I'll give you my credit card, and Alfredo will take you in his pick-up. I'll get Rafael to come in early and cover for him—not that we'll have any business after last night though."

"Why do you say that, Jack? The Ruby's grand opening is over. I'm sure your customers will come back now."

"I wouldn't be so sure." Jack pulled out a sheet of newspaper from his back pocket and handed it to Eden. She gasped when she saw the picture and the caption. It was her flung over Jack's shoulder with her dress hiked up so high she couldn't believe it didn't show more. Her hair was hanging down to Jack's waist, and he had a look on his face she couldn't describe. The caption read "The Golden Talon Goes Neanderthal. Owner Reverts To Violence."

"Oh, Jack, I'm so sorry," said Eden, scanning the story that made Jack out to be some sort of dangerous lunatic who punched Martin Noble in the face for no reason at all.

"Not as sorry as I am," he answered. "If you didn't notice, it's on the front page."

Eden looked again and realized he was right.

He took the paper away from her. "You don't have to read the rest. They mention something I should have told you long ago."

"What's that?"

His eyes were downcast as he crumpled the paper and threw it to the ground. He seemed mad. Mad at himself, and embarrassed as well.

"I never finished school. I'm sure even you had more schooling in your little teaching huts than I've had."

"They're not teaching huts, they're nucleos, Jack. And why should I care if you finished school or not?"

"I had a record of hanging out with the wrong crowd, too," he continued. "I was in some brawls and even did drugs."

"Well, we chew the coca leaf in the mountains to help us deal with the hard life," Eden matched him.

"That's different, honey. What I'm saying is, I'm basically a failure. He had his hands in his pockets, his eyes toward the bean plant. Eden's heart went out to him, and she wanted to take him in her arms, but wasn't sure if the time was right.

"I've lost everything my father has worked so hard to build, and I've disgraced the family name," he continued.

"I understand how you feel," said Eden, and she meant it. "I've disgraced my family's name as well. It actually started when my mother fell in love with an American."

"What's so bad about that?"

"The descendants of the Incas don't marry outside their tribe. My mother became pregnant with me, yet wouldn't marry my father. He came back year after year and spent the summers there. Our summers. After a while he could see he was hurting my mother's image and decided to stay away from her. He only spent time with me. He'd take me up to the Incan ruins of Machu Picchu. I spent the summers with him while he did his research. He taught me English and everything he thought his daughter should know. He even took me to the Amazon and all over Peru."

"That sounds like the professor I knew," said Jack. "Or at least the one I thought I knew."

"He was always so sure he'd find some long lost treasure of the Incas." Eden stared past Jack, remembering her father. "We explored the Temple of the Sun, the Temple of the Moon, he was even certain The Hitching Post of the Sun was some sort of clue."

"Hitching Post?" asked Jack.

"Atop the mountain at Machu Picchu. It's sort of an old-time sun dial."

"Oh. So he never found anything?"

"He didn't," answered Eden slowly. "It's sad that all his time and money were wasted looking for treasure when the real treasure was the love we could have shared if we'd been a true family."

"My money," Jack corrected her.

"What?" Eden blinked, and wondered if she'd heard Jack correctly.

"It was my money he wasted."

Well, she had heard Jack correctly, but couldn't believe it. Jack obviously hadn't let go of the past, and she doubted he'd heard a word she said. He not only blamed her father for the restaurant's failure, but he'd called himself a failure as well. And he looked to money and materiality for happiness. If only he could see how little her people had, and how happy they were. If only he could look past his ego and money issues, and realize she didn't care if he had schooling or not. She cared about him as a person. She didn't care about money. But that seemed to be all that mattered to Jack.

"You'll never learn, Jack, will you?"

"What does that mean?"

"Never mind. I've got a garden to plant. Want to help?"

"I've got something else to do."

Eden's heart fell at his refusal. She had hoped they would get to know each other, yet Jack was running again, just like he always did.

"I'll see you later," said Jack and took off for the garage.

Eden watched as he pulled out of the garage in the convertible and skidded the tires on the stone as he sped away. She tried not to feel disappointed but couldn't help herself. She looked down at the bean plant stretching toward the sun. Jack had planted it without even knowing it. And it had grown into a fine, healthy plant. Maybe she could plant a seed as well. In Jack's mind.

She realized now that her father's gift to Jack to pay back his debt was symbolic. He had never meant the seeds alone would help Jack. No, he had only meant to imply that Jack needed to plant a seed. Well, he would never do it, so Eden figured she would help out. She would find a way to help Jack out of debt, and she knew she'd have to plant a seed to do it.

&

Eden worked till sundown on the garden, not even stopping to eat. It felt good to get back to working with the earth again. She missed it, as well as her family. She brushed off her hands in her skirt and looked around the yard at her creation. Layered terraces in circles and intricate designs made up a pattern throughout the small yard.

She'd put Tisha's kids to work helping her while their mother was resting at home. They dug in the dirt with her, planted seeds, and even helped her put in a few small bushes and a trellis with an archway leading from the garage. The kids had the time of their life and were playing with earthworms when Tisha came to pick them up.

"Thanks so much for watching them all day, Eden."

Eden smiled at Tisha who'd grown bigger with the baby in the last week. "My pleasure. They enjoyed working and did a good job."

"I'll be," said Tisha. "I'll have to try that at home. I thought they were just too young."

"I started working the land as soon as I could walk," said Eden. "It's expected of the young in my culture."

"Well, it's gonna be expected in my culture as well from now on."

"Oh maw," whined Randal. "This is different. We like to get dirty. This is fun."

"Fun," repeated the little one, and Tisha and Eden both laughed.

"What's so funny?" asked Jack, walking up from the garage with bags in his hands. Pink bags. Feminine bags with stripes on them and the name of a girl—Victoria, if Eden wasn't mistaken. He had some white bags also.

"Eden watched the kids today so I could get some rest," said Tisha. "She is so wonderful with them."

"I agree." Jack's eyes interlocked with Eden's, and for a second she wished they were alone. He had that look again. The same look he had when he referred to himself as a big bad wolf. The look like he wanted to eat her. There was an awkward silence for a moment and then he excused himself and headed through the back door.

"You two make a good couple," said Tisha, picking up the baby. "And the way he looks at you is a good thing. Put it this way, it's a blessing to have a good man. Hold on to him Eden, if you know what's good for you. It's hard being by yourself."

Eden knew Tisha's husband had left her and felt sorry for the woman trying to raise her kids by herself, not to mention having another one on the way.

"I'll watch the kids whenever you want me to," she said.

"I appreciate it. Come on, kids, or we're going to miss the last bus home."

"You take the bus with the kids?" Eden hadn't known that. The bus stop was a good four blocks down. Not an easy task for a pregnant woman with three kids in tow.

"I can't afford a car," said Tisha. "I can barely afford the rent."

"What are you going to do when the baby comes? Who's going to watch it while you work?"

"I don't know," answered Tisha softly. "But I pray for an answer every day. I can't afford to pay someone to watch it, and I can't afford not to come to work. Jack's been so good letting my kids stay here. But now—"

"I'll watch your baby for you. When's it due?"

"Why it's due next month. But Eden, I can't pay you."

"You don't need to. Now get these kids home before you miss that bus."

"Mama, Gaspar's missing," cried Patsy. "We can't leave without him."

"I think Gaspar wants to spend the night with me," said Eden. "I'll find him and you'll see him when you come tomorrow."

That satisfied the children, and Eden waved good-bye as they left.

She then headed into the kitchen, wondering why Jack was in such a hurry. He hadn't even stopped to look at the garden and hadn't said what he thought of it either.

She made her way through the kitchen, her stomach grumbling for food. She noticed the restaurant wasn't very busy at all for the dinner time, and she felt bad for Jack. She found the cat hiding under a chair, and scooped it up.

"You can't stay inside the restaurant," she told it. "Jack will have a fit if he sees you in here." She hid the cat partially under her arm and walked past his office.

"Get cleaned up, Eden," said Jack, without bothering to look up. "We're going to dinner."

"We are?" she asked, trying to keep the cat out of sight.

"Wear something nice," he told her. "I'm taking you to the Ninety-Fifth."

Eden had no idea what he meant, and didn't want to stick around to ask. She wanted to get up to the apartment quickly to hide the cat. She no sooner took one step toward the stairs when Jack called out to her.

"And leave Fatso outside."

"Fatso?" she questioned, without turning to look at him. "The cat, Eden. That damned thing has made my kitchen his new home. If everyone would quit feeding him, maybe he wouldn't look like a blimp."

"You're exaggerating," she said, holding the cat up to snuggle it against her face. It mewed loudly and Jack looked up and raised his brows. "Well, maybe he could stand to lose a little weight. Maybe if I kept him upstairs, he wouldn't be eating so much?" she asked with hope in her voice.

"Outside," came Jack's command.

"But I told the kids he'd spend the night with me. How about I put him back outside in the morning?"

"Don't let me find it on my bed," he said. Eden grinned and headed upstairs wondering what to wear on her date with Jack. She couldn't wear the white dress again. Not after the other night. She didn't want to show so much skin again, and she didn't want to tempt Jack. He seemed to be trying to keep his distance and while it bothered her immensely, she respected his decision. He'd said he wanted to start over and that was just what they'd do. But she didn't have any other clothes besides the house dress she'd bought with Ruthie. She guessed that would have to do since her own clothes were too dirty from the garden to wear out to dinner with Jack.

When she entered the room, she spied the bags on the bed. She put Gaspar down next to them, then remembered what Jack said and shooed it to the floor. She opened the bags to peek inside. She found jeans, several t-shirts, button-down shirts, two fancy dresses and one casual. In another bag she found a pair of gym shoes, several pairs of dress shoes, flat, and a half dozen pairs of socks.

Eden laughed out loud at the flat shoes, but thanked Jack silently. He'd even bought her a light-weight jacket and ribbons for her hair. She'd lost her green ribbon shortly after arriving, and was happy to see replacements to hold her braids back. And on the bottom of the bag she found a baseball cap. She really dreaded the thought of not wearing her own hat but knew Jack had hated it all along.

She was on her way to the shower when she saw a box wrapped up in heart paper on the dresser. She pulled the ribbon off carefully, wondering what else Jack could possibly have bought. She gasped when she saw the sexy red floor-length nightgown made from silk and lots of lace. It had thin straps and a plunging neckline and a slit up the side. Then she saw the silk panties and leopard-skin bra. They were so beautiful she didn't know how she could ever bring herself to wear them.

She put them back in the box, stripped off her clothes, and headed for the shower. With any luck, maybe she'd be able to show Jack how they looked on her.

Chapter 17

It was a full month now since Jack had made love to Eden, and it was driving him crazy. He'd taken her to dinner in places such as the Ninety-Fifth restaurant at the top of the John Hancock building and had shown her the city at night. He thought she'd be awestruck by the height, but after living so high up in the mountains it didn't really impress her at all. Instead, she'd told him of the mountain named Huayna Picchu that she'd climbed with her father. Since it was 11,000 feet high, he couldn't top her story.

"And guess what was at the top?" she'd challenged him.

Jack figured it was some sort of temple or Incan artwork carved into the stone. She'd laughed and told him there were temples along the way, but at the top of the world there was nothing but flies.

He liked the way she'd been wearing her new clothes when she worked in the garden and when they dated. She looked good in them and so different from the scared little girl with the big hat he'd first laid eyes on in the cemetery. Once she'd stopped wearing that damned big hat, he could see her face so much better, along with her twinkling blue eyes. The eyes of her father. American eyes. The only attribute about her that gave away her mixed blood.

She was getting accustomed to the States and the North American way of living and they were getting to know each other pretty well. He'd walked hand in hand with her at the Field Museum and even put his arm around her during the star show at the Adler Planetarium. But he hadn't kissed her again since that night. Since the night he'd taken her virginity and part of her soul as well.

Summer was just days away and his father would be coming home soon. He needed to get his mind back on business but just couldn't when Eden was occupying his thoughts day and night. She had turned his back yard into a small paradise of flowers, shrubs, fauna, vegetables, and some things he couldn't even begin to identify. She was great with Tisha's kids and even with that damned stray cat the kids found. And she'd even been making some of her native dishes for the employees to try.

Jack got her whatever she wanted. Even the octopus for the ceviche she'd put together. He never thought he'd like the raw fish dish with onions, marinated with lime juice, but he was wrong. He was beginning to like everything Eden did. He was getting to know the shy woman under the big hat. She was coming out of her shell, so to speak. And with every seed she planted in his garden, she planted one in his heart as well.

He knew he couldn't keep her here forever though. The professor had sent Jack his only child, with hopes he'd help her get home. And although he hadn't sent her home because he was angry at the professor, he had learned to forgive the man and love his daughter. He was becoming too attached to Eden. He was falling in love with her, and he'd never meant for that to happen. Hell, he should have just sent her home the first day he'd brought her from the cemetery. Instead he'd played a game that had gone a bit too far.

He'd buy the ticket. He'd get her home where she belonged. He'd do the right thing to make up for all his mistakes. But he didn't want it to end yet. And she hadn't been complaining to leave anymore. Matter of fact, she seemed to like it here. But he knew she couldn't stay forever. He'd send her home before his father returned.

"Jack? Jack, are you listening?"

Jack hadn't even realized Ruthie was standing in front of him trying to get his attention. He sat at his desk, cigarette in hand. He'd been going over the books and found out he was in deeper trouble than he'd imagined. And the more he tried to save money, the more he spent. With the supplies for Eden's garden, the clothes he'd bought her, and the places they'd gone, he was only getting himself deeper in the hole. And when he added up the bills from the restaurant, he knew he'd never be able to make ends meet.

"What is it, Ruthie? I'm busy." All he wanted was to escape from his worries for a while, or everyone to just leave him alone to think.

"There's a woman here to see you. I think she's a reporter."

Hell and damnation, that was just what he needed. More bad publicity for The Golden Talon. But then again, how could it get any worse?

"What's she want?"

"She said something about doing a special article on our restaurant. She's been interviewing all the restaurant owners around here and she's rating them for some kind of entertainment coupon book that'll be coming out this fall."

"Great. Just another happy thought to fill my day. Do they have such a thing as a negative star rating?"

"Just go talk to her, Jack. She seems like a nice woman."

Jack took a deep drag of his cigarette. "Fine," he said. "Seat her in my usual booth and tell her I'll be out in a minute. Get Alfredo to cook something up and bring it over for her to taste."

"What do you want Alfredo to make for her?"

"Anything he can't burn."

Jack smashed out his cigarette, pushing his ledgers to the side, and headed over to the table. He saw her sitting there, surveying the place. A woman probably in her early sixties, in a business blazer and skirt, cat-like glasses on her face, and her hair pulled tight in a bun. She looked so finicky he figured whatever they served, whatever they did, she wasn't going to like it.

"Hello, I'm Ada Stuart." She extended a hand before Jack could say a word. "I take it you're Jack Talon, the owner of this restaurant?"

"I am." Jack shook her hand and slid into the booth across from her.

"I'm from the Just Entertainment book service. Perhaps you've heard of us. We make coupon books."

"I haven't," he interrupted. "And I've got a full schedule today, so what do you want to know?"

She looked a bit perturbed, but Jack didn't give a damn. She was infringing on his time, he'd call the shots.

"I hear your restaurant is slowly falling apart." She was blunt and to the point.

Slowly falling apart? thought Jack. Quickly was more the word for it, but hell if he'd admit it.

"We're just experiencing a slight set-back. It'll be up and running again in the prime in no time."

"I'll be the judge of that," she bit off. "I've just been over to The Ruby, and I tell you it's quite impressive. It'll be getting the super gold, five-star rating in the report I'm putting together."

Jack ran a weary hand through his hair. "Well, thank you for filling me in on that tidbit of information." He looked around for Ruthie. He needed a drink. "Can I get you a drink Miss Stuart?"

"It's Ms. Stuart," she corrected him. "And no thank you, I don't drink while I'm working."

"Well, I do." He saw Ruthie eavesdropping from the waitress station and since she was making no motion to come to the table, he called to her across the room. "Ruthie. Bring me my usual. No, make it a double."

"Do you always drink so early in the morning, Mr. Talon?" Ada Stuart was looking sternly at him, with her cat-like glasses perched on her nose. She reminded him of his Freshman English teacher, and he felt his stomach churn.

He felt the need for a cigarette and regretted not bringing them with him to the table. "Do you always ask such personal questions, Ms. Stuart? Or are you planning on printing that in your little article as well?"

"What's going on?" Eden popped her head out the kitchen door when she saw Ruthie, Alfredo, and Nathan standing in the waitress station watching something intently.

"Shhhh," whispered Ruthie. "We're trying to hear what Jack is saying."

Eden looked toward the booth and saw a woman sitting there with Jack. Neither of them looked too happy.

"Who is she?" asked Eden.

"A reporter," said Ruthie, straining her ears to hear more. "She's doing a rating on our restaurant."

"And Jack is blowing it," added Nathan. "When he gets done with her we'll be lucky to find ourselves listed at all in that damned book she's making up."

"Well, then we've got to help him," said Eden. "We've got to make this restaurant special so she'll remember it."

"Oh, she'll remember it," said Alfredo. "Especially after she tastes my cooking. She looks like someone who needs to be put in her place."

Eden knew that tone of voice. Alfredo was intending to do something to sabotage the whole thing. She couldn't allow that to happen. She had to do something to help Jack.

"Alfredo, you're not going to cook her anything at all," announced Eden.

"That's the spirit," Alfredo cheered her on. "Let her go hungry."

"I'm going to make her something to eat."

"You?" Alfredo laughed. "You goin' to cook for the old prune?"

"You're damned right," Eden said, surprising even herself at her use of profanity. Hanging around Jack, she was picking up some undesirable habits. "And all of you are going to help me."

Jack was getting impatient waiting for that drink. Ruthie seemed to have disappeared, and he was about ready to get up and pour it himself. Ms. Stuart's nosy questions were making him edgy, and he couldn't wait until she left. And if she kept up with her insults, he'd see to the task personally.

"You seem to have slow service," she noted, writing on her notepad. "And I don't see many customers for so near the noon hour."

"We get a later lunch crowd around here," he told her. "Our customers are unique."

Ruthie walked up with drinks in her hand, and Jack was thankful she'd finally thought to show up. He grabbed the cup of golden liquor from her tray wondering why she was serving bourbon in a tea cup. He figured Eddie was late for work again and they probably didn't have any clean glasses. He downed a swig to try to calm his nerves. He about gagged on the hot contents and would have spit it out hadn't the neighborhood gossip been sitting across from him.

"Ruthie, I wanted a bourbon. What the hell is this?"

"It's called mate, MAH-tay," she over pronounced the word as she gave a cup of it to Ms. Stuart. It's a Peruvian herbal tea. We don't serve liquor before noon."

"Since when?" snapped Jack, wondering who the hell decided that.

"I like that rule," said Ada Stuart as she blew on the contents, taking a little sip of the tea. "Delicious. I've never heard of this before. When did you started serving imported teas?" she asked.

"That's what I'd like to know," growled Jack, looking at Ruthie. She gave him a scolding look, her mouth pursed, her jaw actually still for a change. It was then he realized for once she wasn't chomping on a wad of gum.

Just then Tisha walked up, balancing a tray on her huge stomach. She set a cold plate of ceviche in front of them along with two small plates.

"And what's this?" Ada asked Jack, adjusting her glasses as she eyed up the squid and baby octopus on the platter.

"This is ceviche," Jack told her, using his fork to scoop some on his plate. "It's wonderful, that much I can vouch for. Unless you're opposed to octopus so early in the morning?" He looked at her daringly, holding a dangling octopus leg up on his fork. He then stuck the whole thing in his mouth and watched her eyes bulge.

"Of course not," she said, picking a piece off the plate with her fork, obviously leery of trying it. "I like ethnic food. I take it this is Peruvian as well?"

"It is," said Tisha, bending sideways so her large stomach wouldn't get in the way when she set down the two bowls of soup that came next.

"Mmmmm," said Ada, swallowing and licking her lips. "I never thought I'd like it. That was delicious. I can't wait to taste the soup." She wrote something on her notepad. "Now what is this called?" She picked up her spoon and stirred the contents. The steam rose and fogged up her glasses, so she took them off and laid them on the table, looking quite different from the stern old biddy who had first entered.

"Almuerzo is like a potato broth," explained Tisha. "And your main dish will be up shortly." She and Ruthie left the table with smiles on their faces, something Jack hadn't seen often when they served customers.

What was happening here? Who was making all these changes, and how the hell was Alfredo cooking up Peruvian food that tasted like heaven? Eden had to be behind this. He looked over to the waitress stand and saw Eden peeking out from behind the coffee machine. Her eyes caught his and their gazes interlocked. She looked scared, unsure of herself, and he wanted more than anything to tell her he liked her idea. The woman seemed to feel favorably about the changes, and Jack rather liked them himself. It was what the restaurant needed. New life. New blood. Change.

Eden.

He flashed her a quick smile, wanting to throw her a kiss, but her face disappeared from sight. A moment later he saw the rim of her baseball cap over the top of the coffee machine as she disappeared into the kitchen.

Maybe he'd have to keep Eden around for a while longer. Maybe he wouldn't send her home so soon after all.

❦

"So how'd it go?" Ruthie asked Jack as he pushed through the swinging door into the kitchen.

Eden stood behind the cook's station with Alfredo and Rafael at her side. She was nervous, and Jack's face was so solemn she didn't know what to think. Had she made an impression on the woman, or did she just make more trouble for Jack?

"Eden, I want to see you in my office right now."

He left the kitchen, the door swinging behind him.

"He's mad," said Tisha. "I know that look anywhere. Well, I'm going to go check on the kids outside. I don't want them within shouting distance of him when he starts his cussin'." She wiped her hands on her apron and headed outside.

Eden's face fell as she slowly made her way to the door. She shouldn't have messed with the reviewer. She just should have minded her own business. Tomorrow's headlines were going to be slander about The Golden Talon again, she just knew it.

"Don't look so glum, sweetie." Ruthie popped a piece of gum into her mouth and flipped the wrapper into the garbage. "You did your best. We all did. And I'll be dan-ged, but I could have swore that woman liked her meal."

"I don't think Jack's happy with me, Ruthie. I should have minded my own business."

"Your business is Jack, hon. What he needs is a good woman behind him, only thing is he's too thick headed to admit it. You just go in there and stand up for what you believe. Don't let Jack tell you anything you don't want to hear. I think you were wonderful."

"Thanks, Ruthie." Eden made her way to the office, not at all confident after Ruthie's little pep talk. She didn't want to face Jack now and wished she had her montera on her head instead of the small baseball cap Jack had bought her.

She walked up to the office entrance and stopped when she heard Nathan and Jack conversing in low voices. Then Jack cleared his throat, and Nathan gathered up the books and left.

"Come in," Jack said and walked around his desk.

She entered slowly, pulling the brim of the baseball cap lower over her eyes.

"You wanted to see me?" she asked.

"I do."

"Eden, what you did was out of line. No one goes over my head and makes changes in the menu without asking me first. Especially not when a reviewer is the one eating the food."

He leaned against the desk and crossed his arms over his chest.

Eden knew she should apologize but remembered what Ruthie told her. Stick up for what you believe. She did nothing wrong.

"I was only trying to help you, Jack. And if you'd just give me a second to explain I'd—"

Her words were cut off as Jack pulled her into his arms, ripping off her hat and throwing it across the room. The next moment he had cupped her face in his hands and plastered a huge kiss on her mouth.

"You were saying?" he asked.

Eden found herself too dumbfounded to continue. "I—I don't understand, Jack. I thought you were angry."

"You were brilliant, Eden. She loved the idea of Peruvian food in Chicago, and she's giving us the highest rating, right up there with The Ruby."

"She is?" Eden couldn't believe it. Maybe what she did wasn't so bad after all. Maybe Jack's luck would be changing.

"We've got to get busy," he said and let go of her as fast as he'd grabbed her. "We've got to change this restaurant around before that entertainment book comes out this fall. She's going to be in touch with me about the changes we'll be making.

"Changes?" asked Eden, her head spinning from Jack's whirlwind of sudden energy. "What changes?"

Jack looked at her as if he couldn't believe what he was hearing. "The changes to turn this into a Peruvian restaurant, that's what."

"You mean, with the food and all?"

"Not only the food, Eden. We're going to take every-thing you know about your culture and bring it right here to The Golden Talon. Matter of fact, I think we'll have to change the name." He paced back and forth. "Maybe the Golden Puma or Incan Gold. What do you think? We've got to have a gimmick."

"Will your father approve of this, Jack? After all, he is coming home soon."

"Exactly. And he'll be thrilled when he sees how I've changed it around. Once the money starts rolling in, all he'll see is figures." He picked up his cell phone and pounded out a number. He then sat at his desk, and looked up at her. "You're going to be one busy girl, Eden. I've got plans for this place that'll make me rich."

When he started to talk into the phone, Eden took that as her cue to leave. She made her way to the stairs, not at all sure she was happy about this whole thing.

"Well, what did he say?" Ruthie walked by on her way to serve a table.

"He liked it," said Eden softly. "He's very happy."

In a daze, she made her way up to the apartment. She went inside and closed the door. Everything was happen-ing so fast, it was all so confusing. And Jack was happy. Happy that he'd be making money off the professor's daughter.

She missed her father immensely and wished he was still alive so she could talk to him about all this. She sat on the bed and opened the locket that hung on a chain around her neck. Her father's smiling face was plastered in the left half of the heart. The right half was empty. Just like her heart felt right now.

She looked over to the mirror and saw her reflection. Her Incan face and long braids were being mocked by the Mickey Mouse t-shirt and designer jeans she wore. This wasn't who she was. This was a confused girl trying to be something she wasn't. She belonged back home with her mother. Eden drew a shaky breath. She hadn't even written her mother yet that Jonathan Starke was dead.

She picked up her montera and arranged it on top of her head. Blue eyes—American eyes stared out from within her soul. The soul she no longer knew. Half American and half Incan, not really fitting in either place.

Whenever she was upset, her father used to read to her from the Bible. She'd all but ignored the book since she'd come to stay with Jack. She opened the nightstand drawer and gently lifted out the Bible. She opened it to Genesis and read about the Garden of Eden. The words were comforting, her soul was stilling inside. She felt her father close to her and found solace in her thoughts. Her eyes closed as she tried to still her mind further. Exhausted, she slipped in and out of a light doze. The book fell from her hand and landed on the floor with a thump.

Her eyes flew open, and she reached down to get the Bible. That was when she noticed the lining on the inside back cover was slit and taped back up. She felt the thickness and knew something had been put inside for safe keeping. Probably by her father.

Carefully, Eden pulled back the tape and the lining. An airline ticket fell out, and a folded piece of paper with her name written on the outside in her father's handwriting. She gently unfolded the paper, her heart beating furiously. She was almost afraid to read it, but at the same time longed for her father's words.

He had written in Spanish. She knew he never felt comfortable enough to write in the Quechua language. He'd learned her language and taught her English so they could talk to each other. And for a while, before she became fluent in English, Spanish had been their common ground.

Eden felt tears forming in her eyes and had to bite the inside of her cheek to keep from crying as she read.

Eden, my dear. I write this letter as I lay dying, waiting for you to come to my side. I can only hope I'll live to see your eyes one last time.

As you will find out, I've done something very horrible to a friend. To Jack Talon. He's got the biggest heart of anyone I know. He lent me money to find the treasure of the Incas. A lost treasure which I hoped would bring me wealth and happiness as well. But I never found it, and it still remains hidden.

But I wanted more, Eden. I wanted so much more. I was hoping to use his money to make money for myself. I gambled, hoping to be able to make a large sum and then return to him what I'd borrowed. But in my greed I ruined a man's life. I lost that money and I lost the best friend I ever had as well.

But I want you to know, Eden. I wanted to make that money so I could build a nice place here in the States for you. I know now I was wrong to want to pull you away from your mother. She loves you as I do. And she can teach you what I would have never had been able to. She knows you can't buy happiness, Eden. The Quechua people may live simply, but they are happy.

That's why I used the last of Jack's money to buy you this ticket home. But I didn't tell you about it, because I was hoping you would get to know Jack first before you left. He's a good man, Eden. And you are a good woman. I only wish I could have lived long enough to try to explain this myself. The ticket is here for you, should you decide to go home to your mother. The decision is yours if you'd rather stay with Jack.

Either way, sweetheart, I want you to know I love you. And if I could do it all over again, I would have stayed with you. That treasure I searched for and never found, was really here all along. You are that treasure, Eden. A treasure I've finally found and sadly am about to lose.

I'll love you forever.

Your father, Jonathan Starke

Eden looked at the letter and realized her tears were dropping on the paper and smearing the ink. She picked up the ticket and looked at the date. It was a flight out on August 30th, two months from now. He'd remembered her birthday and made the flight for that date.

Eden was ready to cry some more and probably would have if she hadn't heard Jack knocking on the door.

"Eden! Can I come in?"

She grabbed the ticket and the letter and slipped them both back into the lining of the Bible. She had just closed the book on her lap when Jack poked his head in the door.

"What's going on, Eden? Don't you want me in here?"

"Of course I do." She faked a smile and tried to non-chalantly wipe the tears from her face with the back of her hand.

"You're crying, aren't you?" Jack closed the door softly and came and sat down beside her. "What's the matter, sweetheart?"

"Nothing," she said. "I'm just so happy about your plan to change the restaurant. I think it'll work, Jack. Let's go for it."

Jack thought Eden was the worst liar he'd ever laid eyes on. Something was bothering her, and she didn't want him to know. He saw the tears she tried to wipe away without him noticing. And the Bible her father gave her was on her lap, not to mention the locket with his picture was open on her neck.

"You miss your father, don't you?" He reached out and snapped the locket closed. The back of his hand brushed against her warm skin and sent a spark of fire through him.

"That's right," Eden agreed too quickly. "But I'll get over it in time."

Jack cleared his throat and looked at the hat on her head. It wasn't the baseball cap he had bought her, it was the hat from her native land. She wanted to go home—she was homesick, and he couldn't blame her. He never should have kept her away from her family for so long.

"You want to go home, don't you, Eden?"

She looked up quickly, then lowered her gaze to the Bible on her lap. "No. No, I'm going to stay here and help you with the restaurant. It's the least I can do to pay back my father's debt."

"You don't have to pay it back, sweetheart." He ran a finger over her cheek. "You've showed me that I need to forgive people and stop living in the past. I'll find a way to earn back that money. Maybe with our new food and style, I'll get it back."

"Well, I'll help you, Jack. I'll work off that ticket like you told me I should."

"It would take you a year to earn that kind of money working for me, Eden. I can't even pay my employees or bills."

"That's all right. It was the deal. I'll work for as long as it takes to earn that ticket. And you just get your bills paid up and the employees as well before you even think of paying me."

She was too good to be true. Jack could see how badly Eden wanted to go home, yet she knew he was in trouble and would postpone her trip home in order to help him get out of debt.

"Then maybe we could call your mother. Maybe let your family know you're all right."

"There are no phones where I live."

"But there must be some way to—"

"My people don't worry like Americans do. Life is cheap when you live in the mountains. You get used to disappointment. Most babies don't even live long enough to grow up. And those that do are basically on their own from a very early age. She won't be worrying about me."

"You're just saying that because you feel you're an outcast, aren't you? I'm sure they want you back as much as you want to go."

"I've made my decision, Jack. I'm not going anywhere until I pay back that debt."

He didn't understand her but figured he'd just give her time. Still, he couldn't help but feel he'd done wrong by keeping her here.

"I'll miss you, Eden—when you do go." He ran his hand over her hair and placed a small kiss on her forehead. He wanted to kiss her like he had the other night. He wanted to lay her on the bed and bury himself between her thighs, but he knew he'd only be making their parting more difficult. She belonged with her people, and he had to do the right thing by making sure she got home. But maybe he'd just wait a little longer. Eden said she'd help him make his restaurant Peruvian. And he needed her, or he'd never be able to do it.

Her presence and the fact they were sitting on the bed together was getting his mind racing as well as his libido.

He knew he'd better get out of there fast, not to mention change his thinking before he convinced himself to stay.

"Reading the Bible?" he asked, noticing the way she gripped the book.

"It always helps to clear my mind."

"Then I guess I better take it with me, as my mind needs some clearing itself." He plucked it from her hands and tossed it up and caught it. "The last time I even saw a Bible was in a hotel room in—" He noticed the way she was watching him wide-eyed. "Never mind. You did say you wanted me to have this?" He got to his feet and flipped through the pages. "This and those damned beans, right?"

"I—yes, I did say that."

"Great," he said, snapping the book shut in one hand. "It'll give me something to do when I go to bed. That garage room gets pretty cold and lonely at night."

Eden didn't say anything, and he figured he'd better change the subject before his mind went racing again. "So how about a walk on the beach tonight? After all, it's a beautiful day. First day of summer, you know."

"I—um—that'll be fine," she answered, still looking at the book.

"Good," he said, "and then maybe we can talk more about how to turn our restaurant into an authentic—what's the word you used for nightclubs and restaurants?"

"Peñas," she said, her eyes resting either on the book in his hand or his zipper, he wasn't sure which.

"Peñas," he repeated, but the word just reminded him of the tightening in his groin. "I'll see you tonight, Eden."

He left the room and hoped to hell he could control himself when they walked on the beach.

Chapter 18

Eden brushed her hands on her jeans, admiring the garden she had planted. The vegetable plants were well under way, and many of them would be ready to use in the kitchen soon. She told Jack she'd rather use the vegetables she'd grown herself without fertilizers and pesticides than the store-bought ones. This would be a nice pull to get people into the restaurant. She'd even told him once the garden was in full bloom they should take customers on a tour. Perhaps even let them pick out their own greens or tomatoes for a salad.

Jack was happy, and this made her happy too. But being in her garden also made her long for home. She wondered how her mother was doing. She wondered if little Pia was walking now. She missed them with all her heart, yet she didn't want to go back if it meant having to leave Jack.

She felt good about herself when she was around him. And Jack and his employees accepted her for who she was. She'd never really had friends back home. Besides being treated like an outcast, there was no time for developing friendships. One worked from before sun-up until sun-down. They only socialized on feast days and fiestas and those were too few and far in between.

She liked it in Chicago, but still she longed for the mountains and beauty of Peru. Nothing could compare to the fresh air and wide open spaces. In Chicago, the air was usually foul, the tall concrete buildings threatening to strangle her as she felt so confined.

Eden pushed back her baseball cap and looked at the sky. Dusk was setting in and so was a rainstorm on the horizon. Jack would be looking for her soon, as they had planned to go walking on the beach of Lake Michigan. Maybe that would make her feel better and rid her of this empty feeling within.

She looked up at the room above the garage. Jack's room now. The draperies were closed as they always were, and she knew it was because Jack didn't want her to tempt him. Though they had spent time together and gotten to know each other these past few months, Eden longed to get even closer to Jack. She wanted to relive the night he'd made love to her. But this time she wanted to relax and enjoy it. She wanted it to last longer.

She thought about what Jack said. That he'd be sending her home soon, and this thought terrified her. At one time she couldn't wait to leave Chicago—especially Jack. But now, if he sent her home, she didn't know what she'd do. And he'd taken the Bible with him. The Bible that contained the ticket home. She had to get it back from him before he found it and decided to have her use it.

She quickly looked around, but no one was watching. Tisha and her kids had already left for the night, going back to their run-down apartment in the worst part of town.

She'd have to talk to Jack about that. She didn't feel it was safe for the kids or for a pregnant woman to be living there.

She made her way through the arched trellis and was pleased to see the rose vines shooting up the sides. It would be beautiful when the roses bloomed and the whole trellis sparkled in crimson. She stopped at the foot of the stairs and after one more quick look around the yard, she darted up the steps. She had to get into Jack's room and find that ticket before he did. She didn't want him to know she had the means to get home and wasn't telling him.

She put her hand on the doorknob and turned it slowly, knowing Jack was in the restaurant, but still feeling a bit nervous. This was Jack's personal space, and he hadn't invited her in there. She poked her head in the room and fumbled for a light switch on the wall. When she didn't find one, she slipped inside, leaving the door cracked to let in some light.

Still, it was dark. And damp. She pulled the drapes open just a bit to help her see the surroundings. It was one room. A bit larger than the one room that made up her family's home. A bed came out from the wall, and a chair was pushed near the window. Those were the only pieces of furniture.

She smiled, thinking of the Quechua's way of life. They didn't have much furniture either and used pallets to sleep on. Jack was in a way living like her people. And ironically enough, she was living in luxury across the yard like his people.

She noticed the fireplace on the far side of the room and the logs stacked beside it. She realized the room not only was lacking electricity but heat as well. Then she saw the guitar leaning against the wall. Jack's? She hadn't known he played an instrument. It made her think of her panpipe in her manta. Sadly enough, she hadn't even removed it from her pack the entire time she'd been here.

She was losing her culture more and more every day she stayed here, and this made her sad and confused. She shook her head to clear her thoughts, letting her pony tail swish back and forth. She'd unbraided her hair earlier, liking the way it felt, but even this pointed out that her culture was slipping away. She'd been braiding her hair for the last twenty years, just like the rest of the Quechua women, until she'd come to America. Until she'd met Jack Talon.

Spying a duffel bag poking out from under the bed, she got down on her knees and pulled it out. She realized it was Jack's belongings, what little he'd taken from the room she occupied. What little he needed while living here. She unzipped the bag and looked inside. In Jack's orderly fashion, several changes of clothes were folded neatly and stacked atop each other.

He had extra underwear, socks, a throw-away razor, and a small bottle of the cologne he wore that drove her crazy. Fahrenheit, it was called. And she knew why. Whenever she smelled it on him, her temperature rose. Tucked beside the cologne was a ribbon, bundled up and secured with a rubber band. She recognized the bright green ribbon as the one she'd had in her hair the day she met Jack at her father's funeral. The ribbon she believed lost. He had found it, and kept it.

She smiled, thinking Jack had wanted a remembrance of her, and that made her happy. Maybe he really did care about her after all. And maybe he liked her more than he was letting on.

She dropped the ribbon back into the bag and was digging to the bottom, looking for the Bible, when the door swung open and Jack stood in the doorway silhouetted against a very threatening, stormy sky. A flash of lightning split the sky behind him and thunder rumbled through the air.

Eden jumped to her feet, feeling her heart beating a mile a minute. She leaned casually against the bed post hoping Jack hadn't seen what she was doing.

"I'd ask you if you were digging for treasure," said Jack, "but I know there's nothing of value in my belongings."

"Jack. I didn't hear you coming."

"Obviously not." He sounded so disappointed in her. So hurt that she had gone behind his back.

"Going through my things?" he asked. "Why? If there's something you need, you know all you have to do is ask. What do you want? Money?"

"No." She put her head down, wishing she could hide under the rim of her own big hat. She was embarrassed and ashamed of herself. How would Jack ever trust her again? "It's not what you think," she told him. "I wasn't trying to steal anything of yours. I was looking for something of mine."

Jack closed the door and came toward her in the near darkness. He looked down at her, but she couldn't meet his eyes. He then stooped down, picked up something and took her hand and placed the object in it.

"Here's what you want, Eden. I had no right keeping it. I don't know why I did."

She opened her hand and saw her hair ribbon. She swallowed deeply as Jack went to the other side of the room and threw some logs on the fire. By giving this back to her, it meant to her he was releasing her. That was the last thing she wanted. She had to tell Jack the truth, but didn't want to.

She walked up behind him as he fanned the logs and the glow of the fire lit up the room. He didn't turn to look at her, and she could feel his hurt.

She squatted down next to him and put her hand out, offering him the ribbon. "This isn't what I was looking for."

"Then what?" he asked, making no move to retrieve it. "What was it you wanted so badly that you couldn't ask me for it? That you had to sneak up into my room and go through my personal belongings to steal it from me?"

"I'd never steal from you, Jack, and you know it." She dropped the ribbon on the ground between them. "I only wanted—" She thought about keeping silent, but knew she couldn't. Not if she ever wanted Jack to trust her again. "I only wanted my father's Bible," she blurted out before she could stop herself.

"The Bible?" he asked. "That's what you want?"

She nodded as a flash of lightning split the sky outside the partially open draperies, and a crack of thunder shook the rafters.

"Looks like we'll have to postpone our little walk on the beach." He got to his feet, dropping the subject of the Bible altogether.

"Whatever you say." She didn't know how to bring it up again without seeming too anxious to get it back.

She stood up and made her way over to the guitar in the corner. Picking it up, she plucked a few notes of her Andean folk music.

Jack whirled around. "You know how to play the guitar?"

"No." She sat it back down. "I've learned a few songs on the churrango from my stepfather, but I don't really know how to play."

"Is a churrango like a guitar?" asked Jack.

"It's more like a mandolin made out of an armadillo shell. But I've always liked playing the panpipe better."

"I had no idea." Jack sat down on the bed and kicked off his boots. "Maybe we should have some Peruvian music in the restaurant as well."

"That's a great idea," said Eden. "I think the customers would really like it."

There was silence for a moment as they just looked at each other. The firelight flickered on his face and she couldn't help but think he looked so sexy in his denim shirt and tight jeans. He was staring at her again like he wanted to eat her. That big bad wolf was back, and she welcomed him.

"Come closer," he said in low voice. "I want to look at you better."

She took a step forward and he reached out and held her hands.

"You know, I asked Tisha's kids about that fairy tale you were talking about," she said.

"What fairy tale?" His eyes were locked on her lips.

"The one with the big bad wolf," she said, looking at his own lips.

"Oh. That one." He cocked a half smile. "Well, I guess I should call in the hunter to kill him."

"Don't do that," she said, her voice sounding huskier than she'd intended. "I rather like that big bad wolf."

"So. Are you telling me you'd like to visit him again?"

She laughed. "Well, I'm not here hoping to visit grandma."

Jack reached up and took the cap from her head. He tossed it on the bed, then pulled her closer, positioning her in between his legs. He reached up and took the tie from her hair, letting her long locks fall loose around her.

"I like your hair loose, Eden. It's so long and beautiful."

She liked it that way too, only because it made her feel sexy.

He pulled her into his lap, and she wrapped her hands around his neck. Thunder boomed outside, and rain pelted against the window.

"I've got the night free," he said. "I took it off to go to the beach with you, but now it doesn't look like we're going to make it."

"I guess we'll just have to find something else to do."

"Like what?" he asked, gently placing a kiss on her collarbone. The touch of his lips on her skin made her tingle. It felt so good to have him kiss her again. She reveled in the warmth of his presence.

"Oh, I don't know," she said. "Maybe you could tell me some more fairy tales."

He unbuttoned her shirt one button at a time. She had changed out of her Mickey Mouse t-shirt earlier, and now was glad she did. She liked what Jack was doing. She wanted him to do even more.

"Fairy tales," he repeated, running his hands inside her shirt and around her waist. "Let me see. There's only one I can think of at the moment that I'd be qualified to tell."

He removed his hands from her shirt, a disappointing gesture to Eden.

"What fairy tale is that?" she asked.

He took her hand in his and kissed her fingers. "The one I'm thinking of is Jack and the Beanstalk."

"Really? Well, we've already got the Jack part, now we just need the beanstalk."

"We've got the beanstalk, too, honey. Let me show you." He lay back on the bed, pulling her with him. Rolling on his side, he placed her hand against his male hardness to prove his point.

"I guess we do." She used the advantage to release the snap on his jeans and slowly undo his zipper. Jack seemed to grow beneath her touch. "Can I climb that beanstalk?" she asked.

"It's dangerous climbing beanstalks," he told her. "You never know what you'll find at the top."

"I'm willing to take the risk," she said, rubbing her hand over his length.

Jack had a sharp intake of breath and rolled on top of her. "Are you sure? I still feel bad about the last time."

"Why?" she said. "I don't. And yes, I'm surer than I've ever been. I haven't been able to stop thinking about this ever since the last time, Jack. I know I want you, and I can only hope you want me, too."

"I do, Eden. I want you more than I've ever wanted any woman."

He got off the bed and took off first his shirt and then his jeans. He caught her looking at him when he removed his briefs, and she looked away quickly.

"You have the right to look, sweetie. That's what it's all about."

"Well, you have the right to look, too, Jack." She got off the bed and undressed herself, watching out of the corner of her eye as he lounged on his side, drinking in every one of her moves. She stood before him in her leopard-skin bra and panties, liking the way she felt.

"Thank you for the bra and panties," she said. "I like them."

"So do I," he answered. "I was hoping I'd get to see you in them."

"Not for long," she answered and slipped out of them and stood in front of him naked.

Jack pulled back the covers. She snuggled into his arms and reveled in the feel of his lips on her breasts.

"I'm relaxed this time," she told him. "I'm not a scared virgin anymore. This time I'm going to enjoy it."

"This time I'm going to make sure you do," he answered, pulling her down on the bed, and straddling himself over her, trailing kisses down her neck, around her breasts, and to her navel.

His hot tongue was so tantalizing, he was driving her mad, and she kissed his shoulder and playfully nipped at his arm. He buried his head between her breasts, rolling to one side with her and then back again. She kissed and nipped at him, he did the same to her. She felt the stirring in her core and the wanting for more. She was alive, vibrating, and very much aware of her sexuality. She wound one leg around Jack's thigh and he gripped it, pulling it up higher to rest around his hip.

"I just need to ready you a little better this time," he explained. He reached down between them and ran his fingers through her curly hair. She opened for him willingly this time, and his fingers found a new place to explore. She moaned and stirred and brought both knees up around him. He slipped in and out easily, helped along by her liquid passion. She tried to catch her breath and felt herself climbing, climbing with every stroke. She was experiencing something special and she hoped it would never end.

"Are you ready to climb that beanstalk yet?" he asked.

She couldn't catch her breath enough to answer. The room felt so hot she was sure if he kissed her again her skin would sizzle. He lay down next to her and pulled her atop him as he reached over the bed and pulled something from his jeans on the floor.

"What are you doing?" she asked desperately. She had to have him. Her body was pulsating and she needed to feel him in her now.

"I forgot something."

"What?"

"It's a form of protection," he explained, and Eden knew exactly what he was doing.

When he was ready, she pushed him down on the bed, straddling him with her legs. She rubbed herself against his strong desire and felt him responding even more beneath her.

"I'm ready to climb that beanstalk now." And she did. Lowering herself over him, she climbed to the top of the world. Not even being on top Machu Picchu had made her feel this high. She found a part of her womanhood she'd never known existed. She'd found true pleasure with a man she loved. Jack moved in rhythm with her, calling out her name in ecstasy, and she knew that her climb wasn't a solo.

Chapter 19

Eden awoke in Jack's arms to the sound of thunder. Or at least she thought it was thunder until she realized someone was banging on the door. She lifted her head, her long hair entwining the two of them. They'd slept in each other's arms, made love once again, slept, made love—and each time Jack had used protection. Protection such as that wasn't used much by her people, and she felt uncomfortable that Jack wanted to use it, but she hadn't stopped him.

The banging continued, and this time Eden could hear Alfredo's voice on the other side of the door.

"Señor Jack. Come quick! Señor Jack, are you in there?"

Jack grumbled with his eyes still closed and rolled from his back to his side, wrapping his arms around Eden.

"Aren't you going to answer the door?" Eden whispered in his ear, letting her tongue tease his lobe.

"You keep that up and we'll never get out of this bed today."

Eden rather liked the sound of that, but she heard the urgency in Alfredo's voice and knew they couldn't ignore it.

"Señor Jack! Señor Jack!" Alfredo continued his pounding.

"Do something," Eden said, half sitting in the bed. Jack still had his eyes closed as if it didn't bother him.

"Go away!" Jack shouted to Alfredo. "I'm sleeping!"

"That wasn't nice," Eden scolded.

"Well, he's not nice either the way he woke me up from such a wonderful dream." Jack leaned over and kissed Eden.

"It's an emergency!" Alfredo shouted. "We need you in the kitchen at once."

"Whatever it is can wait till I decide to show up," Jack called. "And I'm not planning on showing my face at least until noon."

"It's Tisha!" said Alfredo. "I think she's having her baby."

"Tisha? Baby! What the hell—" Jack sprang from the bed and pulled on his pants. He struggled with the zipper and Eden couldn't help but notice why. She pushed back the blankets and climbed out of bed, bending over to pick up her bra and panties.

"Egads, woman!" Jack spoke in a low voice. "Don't bend over like that in front of me when I don't have time to enjoy it again."

Eden smiled. "We better hurry," she said, pulling on her clothes.

Alfredo pounded and started to shout again.

"I'll go down first," said Jack. "You come later."

Eden was hurt that he didn't want anyone to know they'd spent the night together, but she didn't waste time arguing. "Hurry, then." She pushed him to the door. "Tisha may need me."

With his hand on the doorknob, Jack hesitated only for a second to look back at her with eyes that said so much, yet he didn't speak a word. In the next instant, he was gone.

When Eden got to the kitchen moments later, Jack had his arm around Tisha, helping her out the door. Tisha breathed heavily and held her hand on her stomach. Her kids ran around their feet playing tag, and Jack stepped on the cat's tail, sending it running for cover.

"I'm taking her to the hospital," Jack told Eden and headed with Tisha for the garage. Ruthie ran out ahead of them, trying to get the kids out of the way. Alfredo was talking anxiously in Spanish to Jack, though Eden knew Jack couldn't understand him.

"Stop that infernal chattering," he told Alfredo, "and help me get her to the car."

"He says she's in labor because she had to carry all her belongings from the bus stop," translated Eden.

"She did what?" said Jack looking at Tisha. "Why in heaven's name would you do a thing like that?"

"I had to," said Tisha, then another contraction made her grit her teeth.

"Will someone tell me what the hell is going on around here?" asked Jack.

"Watch that language around the kids," Ruthie warned him as she tried to stop Randal from hitting Patsy over the head with a loaf of bread. The baby was sitting in the middle of the flower bed crying.

"Like I'm trying to tell you," said Alfredo, and then finished the rest of his sentence in Spanish.

"I can't believe this," Jack mumbled to Eden. "And all I wanted to do today was stay in bed."

Eden smiled when she heard him say that, then looked at Tisha. "Did they really throw you and the kids out of your apartment?"

"First thing this morning," Tisha said as Jack opened the garage door and hauled her inside.

"How did you know that?" Jack asked Eden.

"Alfredo just told us," Eden answered. "You should have been listening."

"I was," grumbled Jack. "A lot of good it did."

"Where are you going to stay now?" Eden helped Tisha in the front seat of the convertible and Jack ran around to the driver's door.

"We can do this small talk later," complained Jack. "I don't take a liking to having a kid born on my front seat. I just had the car detailed."

Eden jumped in the back seat.

"Where do you think you're going?" grumbled Jack.

"I'm coming with you."

"And who's going to watch the kids?"

Eden saw Ruthie struggling across the yard with the youngsters as Jack pulled out. "You go on," Ruthie yelled, "I'll take care of them."

"Put them in front of the TV," Jack called as they drove away in a cloud of smoke. "That always works."

"I think I've got to push," cried Tisha, hands on her belly, and breathing in short spurts.

"Me too!" said Jack. "I need to push this damned gas pedal to the floor, cuz I know nothing about birthing babies."

❧

Jack paced the floor of the emergency room, thankful they'd gotten Tisha into the hospital in time. Tisha had insisted Eden go in the labor room with her, and Jack was now thankful she had come along.

He reached for a cigarette and put it in his mouth when the desk nurse looked up from her phone call and told him no smoking was allowed.

"Figures," said Jack, running a hand through his hair. This wasn't the way he liked to wake up in the morning. This wasn't the way at all.

Eden walked out of the labor room removing a mask and rubber gloves.

"Surgery go all right, Dr. Eden?"

She looked at him strangely, obviously not having a sense of humor.

She came up to him, slipped her arms around his waist, and they shared a kiss.

"I needed that," he said and kissed her again.

"Don't you want to know what she had?" asked Eden, looking so bright and happy as if it was her own joy.

"Gallstones?" Jack smiled and pulled her closer.

Eden hit him playfully with the rubber gloves. "It was a girl, Jack. And she named it after me."

"No kidding! Congratulations." He kissed her again.

"She's beautiful, Jack. You should see."

"I do see," said Jack, looking at Eden.

She blushed. "Tisha doesn't have anywhere to go," she said. "She's got a new baby, four kids, no husband, no money, and no home."

He watched Eden with that little pouty lip and knew she wanted something from him. Didn't everyone?

"What are you trying to say, Eden?"

"I was just wondering if we could fix up the room above the garage for her and the kids to stay in until she gets a little ahead."

"That room's got no electricity or running water, not to mention a toilet."

"Well, then why don't we give her the apartment above the restaurant and we could stay above the garage instead?"

He noticed she was using a lot of we's. He also noticed she was good at getting him to do anything she wanted.

"My father's coming back soon, Eden. He'll need to use the apartment. I can't give it to Tisha and the kids."

"Then how about that room over the garage?" she asked again.

"That'll mean having to hire someone to fix it up." And that would mean getting himself further in debt, though he didn't want to sound heartless and say this.

"How soon can they have it done?" she asked.

"Well, Nathan's brother does construction, and he's got an uncle who does both electric and plumbing. Maybe if I talk to him—"

He didn't get a chance to finish. Eden was jumping up and down and plastering his face with kisses.

"Oh thank you, Jack. I can't wait to tell Tisha. She's going to be so happy."

Eden rushed off down the hall and disappeared. Jack ran his hand through his hair and wondered how we was ever going to afford it.

"Why do I keep getting myself into these situations?" He had only one thing he could sell to make enough money to fix up the place for Tisha and the kids. And he wasn't going to have an easy time letting go of his car.

Chapter 20

Eden was thrilled with the way the room over the garage had turned into a two-bedroom apartment with bathroom almost overnight. The doctor kept Tisha in the hospital a few extra days as she was suffering from exhaustion and he wanted to keep a close eye on her. But today was the day Tisha would bring the baby home, and Eden had involved everyone at the restaurant in a special welcome-home party for Tisha and Baby Eden.

"Your mama is going to be so surprised at the little party we planned for her," Eden told Patsy as she picked one last flower from her garden to add to the bouquet.

"So I have another sister?" asked Patsy.

"You do," she told her with a smile. Patsy looked a little jealous, and Eden knew it wasn't going to be easy for the little girl. "You're the biggest girl in the family, Patsy. And you'll have an important job showing the baby around your new house."

"I'm glad I'm going to be living here by you," she said. "I like you. I like Jack too. When are you going to have a baby?"

Out of the mouth of babes, she thought. The exact question had been on Eden's mind too, since she was late with her cycle. Ever since the night she'd lost her virginity, she had somehow known something was different inside her. Could she be pregnant with Jack's baby? And what would she do if she was? Well, she didn't have time to think about that right now. Right now there were things to be done.

"You go give these flowers to Ruthie to put in a vase," said Eden. "And tell Uncle Jack it's time for us to go pick up your mama and the baby from the hospital."

"Okay," said Patsy smashing the flowers as she grabbed them and skipped down the stone pathway that led through the arbor.

"Whoa," said Jack as he bumped into the little girl in the archway. "Slow down, killer." He sent her on her way, then looked at Eden. "What's this I hear? You're referring to me now as Uncle Jack to the kids?"

"Well, if we're all going to be living here like one big family, they have to call you something."

He stopped in front of her and gave her a kiss. "The garden looks beautiful, Eden." He handed her a rose. She recognized it as one from her garden, but the thought of his romantic gesture made her smile.

"Thank you, Jack."

Jack looked up at the room above the garage and the workers who were just finishing up. Nathan had been wonderful and brought a whole crew so the job would be done before Tisha got back. Only problem was, it cost him more than he'd planned to spend. He bought all new appliances for Tisha, trundle beds for the kids, not to mention he bought a big screen TV and a neighbor's second-hand computer loaded down with educational software for the kids. But they deserved it. Tisha always helped him out in a bind, and now that she didn't have a man in her life, he only wanted to help her out as much as he could. But damn, he wished he hadn't had to sell the convertible to do it.

"We should get going," said Eden. "Where'd you hide the car? I haven't seen it in the garage the past few days."

"I'm not driving, Eden. I've got a friend coming to take us to the hospital."

A horn beeped in the alley. Jack took Eden's elbow and escorted her toward the sound.

She saw Missy sitting behind the wheel of Jack's convertible and didn't understand at all what was going on.

"Missy, what are you doing driving Jack's car?" she asked. "And where have you been lately? I haven't seen you since the night of The Ruby's grand opening."

Giggling, Missy took off her sunglasses. "It's my car now, Eden. I bought it from Jack."

"Your car?" Eden looked at Jack, then back at Missy.

"We'd better go before we're late," said Jack. He opened the door, and Eden climbed in the back. She figured Jack would sit in front with Missy but instead he smashed his tall frame into the tiny back seat with her.

Missy stepped on the gas, almost giving Eden whiplash the way she spun the tires. Eden noticed the cringe on Jack's face and the urgent way he was patting his pocket for a cigarette, though he couldn't find one.

"So why did you sell your car?" Eden asked Jack.

"A man does what he needs to do." He kept a stone face, and although his arm was around the back of the seat behind her, he stared out in the opposite direction.

"He said he needed the money for something more important." Missy looked back and forth in the rearview mirror as she spoke.

"Oh, Jack!" Eden felt as if her heart had dropped into her stomach. "Don't tell me you sold your car to make the room for Tisha?"

"Okay, I won't tell you."

Suddenly Eden felt horrible. It was all her suggestion they help Tisha, but she didn't know Jack would have to sell his car to do it. She never meant for that to happen. But it was too late now to do anything about it.

"How'd Jack know you needed a car?" Eden asked Missy.

"Nathan told him. Nathan and I are dating now, you know."

"I didn't know," said Eden. "What does Martin say about that?"

"Not much he can say when he's in jail," stated Missy.

"Jail! What happened?"

"He was using me, Eden. He only wanted me for my money. And I'm just glad Nathan saw what was going on and had me back out of the deal with Martin. They found he was running an illegal drug ring right from the back room of The Ruby."

"How come I didn't know about this?" asked Eden. "Jack, why didn't you tell me?"

"I only just found out about it myself, Eden. Seems the big bust came the day we took Tisha to the hospital. Too bad I missed it. I would have loved to seen Noble's face when they hauled him away in cuffs."

"Well, I guess The Ruby won't be getting that good review after all," said Eden.

"They've closed it down until they can further investigate," Missy informed them.

Eden knew this would bring Jack so much more business. All The Ruby's customers would now be coming across the street to eat instead.

"That's good news for us, Jack, isn't it?"

"We'll see," was all Jack said and just kept staring in the other direction.

✺

The welcoming party for Tisha's baby had gone well, and Eden couldn't stop holding the little cutie. She'd told Tisha she'd be happy to baby-sit—all her kids, and had tied her manta on her back and put the baby in it, showing Tisha how they carried babies back home.

Jack was a bit quieter than usual, and Eden wondered if he was getting worried. The end of summer wasn't far away, and his father would be coming back soon.

The business had been picking up slowly but surely, and the customers seemed to like the idea of Peruvian food. But they still had so much to do before they announced The Golden Talon's grand opening. There

were walls to paint, chairs to re-upholster, and they need-
ed to do an overall decorating job to make it look Peruvian.
And Eden knew all these things cost money. Money that
Jack no longer had.

Missy was still loaded with money and offered to give
Jack a loan. His male pride obviously was the only thing
stopping him from accepting.

They all worked hard day and night. Eden was mostly
kept busy with the kids, since Tisha was supposed to be on
bed rest for a while. Eden didn't mind, but it was taking
away from her time with Jack. And he'd been so preoccupied lately that she wondered what was bothering him.

They'd been sleeping in the same bed every night, yet
they only made love about once a week. Each time, Jack
made sure they used protection, but she still wasn't comfortable with that habit. Most of the time, though, they
were both so tired that they fell asleep even before their
heads hit the pillow.

The summer flew by, and as the seeds in Eden's garden
grew and flourished into beautiful plants, Jack's seed within her grew as well. She was certain now she was pregnant,
and when she bought a home pregnancy test and saw the
results, she was excited, frightened, and confused all at the
same time. She knew she had to talk to someone before
she burst from trying to keep the secret, but she didn't
know who to trust. She didn't want to tell Jack yet. He had
so many other worries on his mind with the restaurant and
his father coming home next month. Plus, she wasn't
showing yet, so she figured she would wait. She would just

wait until they were having an intimate moment together. Until the time was right.

🐛

Jack stood in his office staring at the airline ticket to Peru he had bought for Eden. He was no longer sure he'd done the right thing. When he bought the ticket over a month ago he believed he'd be happy to be doing what the professor wanted him to. He wanted to do the right thing, and this was the only way he knew how.

He was never one to care about doing what was expected. Or at least not until his father gave him the chance of a lifetime to make something of himself. Now he had the whole world in his hands—just not Eden's world as well.

He'd grown to love her in the short time she was in his care. He no longer wanted her to leave. But she had a family in Peru. A mother, siblings, people she loved. And she could never go back to them unless Jack bought her that ticket.

He sat in his desk chair, swiveling back and forth, just staring at the ticket in his hand. He'd made it for the end of September. Right before his father was to return. Was it a subliminal fear that made him do that? Didn't he want his father to know about Eden? He knew Alastair Talon would never accept Eden and never accept the fact his only son had fallen in love with a girl who had nothing and lived in such a primitive country, with a primitive culture of which she was proud.

"I did what I had to," he said to himself. He threw the ticket on the desk and lit up a cigarette, wondering whom he was trying to fool. He then threw the pack of smokes on top of the ticket to Peru.

"Who you talkin' to, Jack?" asked Nathan, entering the office.

"Someone who no longer exists."

"What's that mean?" Nathan sat his butt on the desk and grabbed a cigarette from the pack, eyeing the ticket in the process.

"I'm not the same Jack Talon I was a few months ago." Jack ran his hand through his hair and took another drag from the cigarette, blowing the smoke in the air.

"Does that statement have anything to do with the airline ticket sitting on your desk by any chance?"

Jack picked it up and looked at it, propping his feet on the desk and leaning back in his chair.

"This has everything to do with it."

"I see." Nathan nodded his head in thought. "You sending Eden home?" Nathan seemed as shocked as Jack was that he would do such a thing.

"I'm only trying to do the right thing."

"I see." Nathan took a few puffs of his cigarette, and the two of them sat there for a minute in silence. "She know about this?"

"Not yet."

"When you plan on springing it on her?"

"Don't know. But the ticket is for the end of September. So sometime before then."

"I see," Nathan said again, and Jack was getting unnerved.

"What do you see?" he asked. "And why the hell don't you stop saying that?"

"What I see is a man who is in love with a wonderful woman but is too damned stubborn to admit it. You think by sending her home you'll make up for all the wrong you've done. That you're going to redeem yourself by putting Eden back in the mountains where she belongs."

"Damn it, Nathan! I'm just trying to do the right thing here. The professor told her I'd get her back home, and I've got to honor the man's dying request."

"Even if it tears you apart in the process?" asked Nathan. "And what do you think it'll do to Eden when she finds out you no longer want her?"

"She's got a family at home, Nathan. She wants to go back."

"So sure are you? What makes you think Eden's not in love with you just like you're in love with her?"

Jack threw the ticket on the desk and jumped to his feet. "What the hell is all this talk about love, Nathan? And since when did you become such a damned expert on the subject? Did Missy put that lame idea in your head or what?"

"Just askin'," said Nathan coolly. "And just callin' the shots as I see them."

Nathan put out his cigarette and headed for the door.

"Don't say anything to Eden about this," Jack pleaded with him.

"That's your job," Nathan answered. "Good luck." And he headed out the door.

"What shouldn't he tell Eden?" came a voice Jack recognized only too well.

He looked up to see Eden standing in the open doorway. His eyes shot over to the ticket and then back to her. His heart raced. He couldn't let her find it. Not just yet. He tried to be casual as he opened the desk drawer and scooped in the papers that were cluttering up the top, slamming the drawer shut and trying to look natural.

"Eden. I didn't hear you coming." He hoped she didn't notice what he had done.

"You're hiding something from me, Jack Talon. Now what is it?"

"Me? Hide? I was just talking over some plans with Nathan, that's all." He smashed his cigarette out in the ashtray.

"Oh, I think I know what it is," she said and sat on his lap and put her hands around his neck. He put his arms around her waist and pulled her closer, liking the way her body felt so close to his. She must know he'd bought the ticket, but she didn't seem upset at all. But Jack was upset with himself and had to explain to her why he'd done it.

"Oh, hell, Eden. I hope you're not upset. I was only trying to do the right thing."

"Upset?" she asked and laughed. "Why should I be? I'm thrilled."

Well, maybe she didn't want to stay with him after all. And maybe Jack was beating himself up over nothing that meant anything to Eden.

"Ruthie told you my birthday was coming up, didn't she? I bet you're planning some sort of big surprise party and just don't want me to know."

"Birthday?" asked Jack. She thought he had done something for her birthday? Hell, he hadn't even the faintest idea when it was.

"Don't try to pretend you didn't know my birthday is on the same day you set for The Golden Talon's grand opening. I bet that's why you chose August 30th, wasn't it? You sly devil." She played with his hair and gave him a small kiss on the nose.

"I thought we chose that day because it was the feast day of Santa Rosa of Lima, some big fiesta day in Peru. Not to mention it was a weekend and a good time to do business."

"Jack, you are such a kidder. I'll play along if you want and pretend I don't know a thing."

She didn't, Jack realized. And hell if he would tell her about the ticket now. He'd just wait till later. Until he had planned a party for her. After all, he couldn't disappoint her when she had told him she was expecting one, could he? And there was still time.

"So what do you want at this little party of yours, Eden?" Jack loved the way Eden got excited, her blue eyes lighting up and her cute little mouth curving in a mischievous smile. Even those braids looked cute on her now.

Something Jack thought he'd never get used to. But at least she wasn't wearing that damned big hat of hers. That was where he drew the line.

"Well, in Peru we have all sorts of entertainment from la corrida, to horse racing, to cockfighting at festivals.

"No horse racing in here," said Jack. "And the only cock I know of doesn't want to fight."

"Jack." She hit him playfully in the arm and blushed. Her cute little rump was squirming on his lap and making him hard. And he knew Eden would notice.

"And what the hell is corrida?" he asked.

"Bullfighting," she said with a smile. "Out of the question?"

"I get enough bull from my employees, I don't need more."

She looked at him strangely, and he figured his joke went over her head. "What else you got?" he asked, shifting her so her legs straddled his waist. He pulled her closer and buried his face in her chest.

"Not now, Jack. We've got work to do first. We need to plan this grand opening before your father returns."

Jack knew she was right and turned her around and set her feet on the floor. He then got up and paced the room.

"We can set up a sapo in the back of the dining room," Eden suggested. "That is, if you don't think it's going a bit too far."

"Well now, that all depends," said Jack. "What is a sapo?"

Eden laughed and put her arms around him, squeezing him in a hug. "Sorry, Jack. When I get excited I sometimes slip into the Quechua language, forgetting you don't know it. Sapo means toad."

"Toad?" Jack hugged her and looked down into her big blue eyes. "First you want horses, then cocks and bulls, and now you want toads?"

"It's not a real toad, Jack. It's a game. You use a large metal toad with its mouth open. Everyone takes turns tossing disks to see who gets the closest. The one who gets the disk inside the toad's mouth scores the highest."

"Not a bad idea. Now we just need to find someone to play the part of the toad. Maybe we can get Nathan for the part, he's pretty ugly. No warts though as far as I know."

Eden's laugh filled the room and also lightened Jack's heart. She was the happiness he needed in his life, yet in another month he would send her away. He looked over to the desk where the ticket lay hidden. No, he thought, he wasn't at all sure about anything anymore.

Chapter 21

Jack looked around the restaurant at the wonderful transformation that had taken place in the last few weeks. The place looked like a page right out of the travel encyclopedia depicting the life and style of the mountain people of Peru.

It was the first night of the chica fiesta, which Eden told him, was a week of more or less total partying, playing music, eating—the works.

Business had picked up immensely since Martin Noble's place was shut down. And when Ada Stuart's coupon book came out a month early with The Golden Talon's six-star rating listed, people were waiting at the door at opening time. Ada had added an extra star, or made it up actually, right after her last visit when Eden had played the panpipe and Jack strummed along on the guitar. Of course, the fact that Jack gave her flowers probably helped the matter some. He was so happy, he could have kissed the old biddy, but just smiled and kissed Eden instead.

For some reason Eden had been wearing only skirts lately and not those snug-fitting jeans that kept looking better and better on her all the time. She even came up with the idea that the waitresses should wear the native costume. Of course Jack drew the line when she suggested they braid their hair and wear tall white hats.

Jack looked at his restaurant and how it had flourished since the first time he'd laid eyes on the girl from Peru. He then spotted Eden across the room, greeting customers in the Quechua language, napaykullayki, hello.

"She's amazing, isn't she?" Ruthie walked up in a bright pink skirt and short black jacket. Jack actually thought she looked pretty good, especially since she no longer chomped on gum anymore. Eden had worked with her on her food cravings, and now Ruthie ate only at mealtimes.

"Yeah, that new hostess we hired is working out well," said Jack, teasing Ruthie.

"That's not who I'm talking about, Jack, and you know it."

"Who then? The new waitresses? They're not doing a bad job either."

Jack's business had picked up so much he even had to hire more people to work the floor. Alfredo had come to him and told him he had family from Mexico coming to live with him who needed jobs. Jack not only hired Alfredo's mother as hostess, but his six sisters as waitresses and his cousin to help in the kitchen. And since the cousin was helping out, Alfredo hadn't burned a thing.

Jack had explained to Alfredo he couldn't pay them much right now, nor give him that raise he'd promised, but Alfredo said it didn't matter. He was just happy Jack gave them jobs.

"I think Eden fits in nicely, don't you?" asked Ruthie. "Tisha's kids love her, and she's a wonder with Alfredo's family since most the rest of us don't know a word of Spanish."

Ruthie was right. Jack didn't know what he'd do without Eden. But he had the ticket sitting in his desk drawer, even though he still hadn't told her he planned on sending her home in just a little over a month.

"What's the matter, Jack?" Ruthie hit him on the arm to get his attention. "You seem so distant lately. Aren't you happy Eden helped you turn this place around? Your father will be so proud he'll be busting buttons on his coat. He'll give this place to you now, Jack. There's no doubt about it. Doesn't that make you happy?"

Jack nodded his head slightly. "Yeah. I'm happy," he told her in an unconvincing voice.

"Sure doesn't sound like it, Jack. You sound tired. Maybe you haven't been getting enough sleep lately? Since you moved in with Eden?" Ruthie winked and walked over to take an order at a table.

Jack knew he should be happy, so why did he feel miserable? He reached into his pocket for a cigarette, half noticing the large group of women coming through the front door. He saw them talking with his new hostess, then Eden joining them. He walked a bit closer, sticking the cigarette into his mouth. That's when he overheard what they were saying to Eden.

"I'm the president of a romance writer's critique group," said a shorter woman with short, dark hair. "We're looking for a restaurant to meet at afterwards, every Wednesday night."

"Really?" asked Eden. "Well, I think you'll find The Golden Talon the perfect place to socialize."

"Well, that all depends," said the woman. "Is this a non-smoking restaurant? We'd really prefer one."

Jack stopped, struck the match and held it to his cigarette.

"Yes," he heard Eden tell her. "We've been changing a few things, getting ready for our grand opening. This restaurant is now non-smoking only."

"Really?" he heard the woman ask with a hint of sarcasm in her voice.

Jack stopped in mid-motion, the flame centimeters away from his cigarette. He didn't need to look up to know his timing was off. Way off. But when he did, fifteen pairs of eyes stared at him in silence. One big blue pair in particular.

"Aw, hell," he said aloud. "Eden, I don't think—"

"Every Wednesday night," she reminded him. "They're a rather large group."

"We have more members joining every day," the woman told Eden. "This is actually a small gathering tonight."

Jack looked at Eden's pleading eyes, then back to the rest of the women awaiting his answer. He knew a regular group of this size is exactly what the restaurant needed. He also knew women talked, and word would get around fast that The Golden Talon was a non-smoking restaurant.

Good, free promotion. But he needed his smokes. They calmed him down, and with all the stress he'd been under lately, there was no way in hell he was going to give them up.

The match burned his fingers and he dropped it to the ground, stamping out the flame and shaking his hand in the process. The women still stared at him, and Eden was giving him that cute little pout, whether she realized it or not. How he hated being in these type of situations. Hadn't he changed enough already?

"Well, are you going to seat them or not?" he asked Eden. "After all, a non-smoking restaurant is a busy place, so you'd better grab a table before they're filled."

Eden flashed him a look of gratitude and directed the large group to follow her to their table. Jack just looked on, the unlit cigarette still dangling from his lips.

"That was big of you, Jack," said Ruthie from right behind him. He turned toward her and she snatched the cigarette from his mouth. "Think you'll survive?"

"With Eden making changes, I doubt it. That girl will be the death of me yet."

"If you didn't care so much for her, you wouldn't talk that way, Jack. Here." She handed him a pack of gum. "I don't need this anymore, but I think you will."

He blindly took the gum as Ruthie headed off to wait on the romance writers' table. He walked into his office, feeling himself weakening, changing. Same thing in his opinion. He tried to clear a space for his feet on his too cluttered desk. A desk that had always been spotless, before all this damned change in his life. He pushed some of the paperwork aside, noticing Eden's Bible under a huge stack of papers.

"That's where I put it." He fished it out and, leaning back in his chair, he opened it up. Eden had been asking him about it constantly, but he honestly hadn't remembered where he put it. It was important to her for some reason. So important that she was willing to break into his room and nose through his duffel bag trying to find it.

Jack flipped through the pages, read a couple verses, and was ready to toss it back in the mess on his desk when he saw a paper sticking out of the back cover lining.

Jack put his feet on the ground and made a quick scan out the door to make sure no one was coming before he pulled out the paper. It was a letter with Eden's name on it. It was all written in Spanish, so he couldn't begin to read it. He noticed it was signed by Jonathan Starke and figured it was just some old letter. He was jamming it back into the lining when he realized it wouldn't go back in until something else came out.

He grabbed his letter opener and pried out an airline ticket. His heart beat faster as he put down the opener and looked inside the envelope. It was a ticket for next weekend in Eden's name. A ticket for her to return to Peru.

He was hurt, thinking she somehow got hold of a ticket and didn't even tell him. She did want to go home, but she was pretending she didn't for some unknown reason. Then he noticed the postmark on the envelope and realized the address on the front was Jonathan Starke's.

Suddenly everything made sense. Her father had a ticket for her to go home all along, but he'd hidden it in the Bible, not wanting her to find out until later. But why? There had to be some good reason.

"Hola, Jack." Rafael walked by the open office on his way to the kitchen to start his shift.

"Rafael, come here!" called Jack.

The man entered the room. In the time Rafael had worked for Jack, he'd never been called into the office for anything. Alfredo practically lived in there, but this was new to his cousin, and Rafael seemed to think he was in trouble.

"Did I do something wrong?" he asked.

"No, no. Not at all. Have a seat. Relax."

Jack had to know what was in that letter. And he couldn't ask Alfredo, because he knew Alfredo would tell Eden all about it. Rafael was different. Jack thought he could keep his mouth closed.

"I just wanted you to read something for me. Something in Spanish," Jack explained.

"Oh, is that all!" Rafael sat back and smiled.

Jack held out the letter, his hand shaking a bit. He hoped to hell Eden didn't stick her head in the office while Rafael was spilling all her precious secrets.

"This letter is to Eden." Rafael looked up with questioning eyes.

"I know. Look, Rafael, I need to know what it says. And you have to promise me you won't tell Eden I found it and asked you to read it."

Rafael just nodded slightly and started to read the letter.

When he'd finished, everything made perfect sense to Jack. And he now knew exactly what he had to do.

"Thanks, amigo," Jack smiled and took the letter.

"Sure, Jack." Rafael got up and left.

Jack was just putting the letter and ticket back into the lining of the book when Nathan walked in.

"What's up, Jack? Reading the Bible? Wow, has Eden changed you!"

Jack fixed the lining the way he'd found it and slammed shut the book.

"I know what to do about Eden, Nathan."

"I thought you'd already decided that. That's why you bought her that ticket home."

"I've changed my mind," Jack said.

"So, you're letting her stay? I don't understand."

"I found a pre-dated airline ticket with her name on it in the Bible. Her father put it there along with a letter before he died."

"So what are you getting at, Jack?"

"The professor liked me, Nathan. He wanted his daughter to marry me. He wanted me as a son-in-law, but he wanted Eden to decide for herself whether she wanted to go or stay."

"I don't get it," confessed Nathan.

"She knew about this ticket for a long time," Jack told him. "That's why it was so important for her to get this Bible back."

"She was going to leave and didn't want to tell you?"

"Just the opposite. I think she wanted to stay and didn't want me to find this ticket and send her home."

"How can you be sure, Jack? This is kind of a long shot isn't it?"

"Not any more of a long shot than I'm about to take right now."

Jack put the Bible on the desk and picked up the phone.

"Who're you calling?"

"The airline."

"Jack, you've lost me coming and going here."

"I'm calling to get another ticket to Peru."

"But you've already got two of them for the girl. Why the hell do you need another one?"

"This one's not for Eden," Jack explained. "This ticket is for me."

Chapter 22

It was the night of the grand opening and also Eden's birthday. Eden had gone with Jack to breakfast, and then they'd spent most of the morning on the beach. She decided not to wear the bikini Jack bought her. She couldn't, without him noticing her stomach. She was starting to show now. She'd worn a one-piece bathing suit instead and kept the wrap-around skirt on all day.

They had been so busy with chica fiesta week, and Eden had been so tired lately that she'd been denying Jack's advances, wanting to make love. Actually, she could have found the strength but didn't want Jack to notice the bulge of her tummy. She was going to tell him tonight. Right after the birthday party he was throwing for her. Right after the restaurant closed and they'd gone up to the apartment to spend the night together.

Jack had told her he had a surprise for her. And she had told him she had a surprise as well. Her stomach was topsy-turvy all day, and she couldn't eat. She was so nervous and excited and only hoped Jack would be excited as well when she told him her little secret. She'd kept this secret for way too long. Only Tisha had known, and she made Tisha swear she wouldn't tell Jack.

"Happy birthday again, sweetheart." Jack walked up in the middle of a busy restaurant and kissed her with so much passion she thought they'd have to call the fire department to put out the flames.

"Save that for later, Jack." She pulled back and smoothed down her thick braids.

"Not a hair out of place," Jack teased her and tweaked at her rump, making her jump. "You're a bit jumpy tonight, Eden. Anything wrong?"

"No. Just nervous about that surprise you have for me. And about the one I have for you. Am I going to like yours?" she asked.

"I don't know," he said. "But I hope so. Am I going to like mine?"

She felt a tingle go up her spine, and she prayed to God he would. She didn't know what she'd do if he was angry that she was pregnant, or if he didn't want a baby. Or if he didn't really want her either.

"We'll find out tonight, I guess." Eden did her best to smile naturally. She toyed with her locket around her neck. "Thanks for the photo of you for the locket. You're right in there with my father."

"I didn't want that heart of yours half empty," he told her. "I hope you like it."

She did like it. Immensely. It felt good and secure to have Jack so close to her heart. He had filled the empty spot in her locket as well as her heart.

"How bout I challenge you to a game of frog?" he asked.

Eden laughed and rubbed his arm. "It's called sapo, toad," she corrected him, noticing the twinkle of mischief in his eye. Oh Jack, you always know how to make me smile."

"Jacky boy!" called a deep voice from the entrance.

Jack knew that voice anywhere. And it wasn't one he'd heard in a long while. Anxiety overtook him as he slowly turned toward his father. What was he doing here now? He wasn't supposed to be back for another month yet. His father was smiling. That was a good sign. So maybe he'd like the changes Jack made in the restaurant after all.

"Who's that?" asked Eden. "Another old friend?"

"No, Eden. That is Alastair Talon. That is my father."

Eden let go of his arm, but he took her hand and put it back. He wanted her at his side when he talked with his father. He wanted to show Eden off to the whole world. After all, she was the one who saved his ass. She was the one who'd turned around the restaurant, not to mention his life.

And after tonight, everyone would know the girl from Peru as Mrs. Jack Talon. Or at least he hoped Eden would say yes when he asked her to marry him. He'd decided she was his world, and he wouldn't have her going back to her world without him. He'd called the airlines and they were going to mail him his ticket. He would give the other ticket to Eden tonight and explain his was coming later. He would take her back to visit her family one last time before she moved here with him to help him run The Golden Talon.

"Come on, Eden. I want you to meet him."

Jack walked up to his father with Eden on his arm.

"The place looks great, Jack!" His father slapped him on the back, then embraced him. "I knew all along you could do it. You have it in you to be a businessman. From what I see here, I can honestly say I'll have no regrets giving you the restaurant."

"Jack! You did it," said Ruthie. "Congratulations." She then greeted Alastair Talon, blushing a bit when he didn't recognize her at first in her new attire. Ruthie was the only one left of the old employees. But when Jack's father had run the restaurant, Ruthie was nothing but part of the maintenance crew.

"Isn't that wonderful!" said Eden, squeezing Jack's arm. "You own your own restaurant. You've got your dream after all."

It was all happening so fast, Jack didn't know how to stop it. Before he could tell his father his plans, the word was out that he was the new owner and people kept coming up and congratulating him.

"Dad, I have someone I want you to meet. This is Eden Ramirez."

His father barely looked at Eden, just nodded his head and muttered that he was glad to meet her. This bothered Jack immensely, and Eden seemed a bit uncomfortable as well.

"She's from Peru," Jack started to explain.

"How nice, Jack. We could use some authentic help in the kitchen. Now let her get back to work because I found someone on the plane ride home that I think you'll be interested in seeing."

He put his arm around Jack and escorted him away from Eden. Jack looked back at Eden. She had her arms crossed over her chest and her head down. He wanted to go back and get her and explain to his father that he loved her, but he didn't want to disappoint his father when he had a guest for Jack to meet.

"Ginny, come on in."

Jack's mouth dropped open when he saw Ginny Valmouth, his old girlfriend walk into the room in an all-out sexy dress and a bottle of champagne in her hand.

"Congratulations, Jacky baby," she said, and before he could stop her, she'd kissed him on the mouth. Jack took out his handkerchief and wiped away the excess lipstick. He glanced at Eden who looked like she was about to cry.

"I figure now that you'll be a prospering restaurant owner, you'll need a sexy wife to keep you in your place," said his father. "I hear Ginny wants you back. She's already told me she's sorry for leaving. She was on her way back to propose to you."

"Dad, we have to talk," Jack tried to ignore the woman who was once his fiancée. Things were different now, and he no longer wanted her. He didn't want any woman but Eden.

Ginny put her arm around Jack's waist, and she and his father hustled him to the other side of the room. Far away from Eden and much too close to Ginny Valmouth.

Eden watched Jack's father and a beautiful woman she didn't know take him away from her. She didn't understand what was going on but figured she could ask Jack about it later that night. If she'd overheard right, Jack's dad said Ginny wanted to marry him.

Ruthie walked by, and Eden stopped her.

"Ruthie, who is that girl with Jack?"

Ruthie turned, straining her neck to see who Eden was talking about. "Oh that's Ginny. Don't let her bother you. She's just Jack's ex-girlfriend."

"Girlfriend?" Eden asked. "Were they serious?"

"I thought so," Ruthie said. "But when she found out Jack was a drop-out, she dumped him like a hot potato."

"I had no idea."

Eden looked over to where Alastair Talon was ushering Jack into the booth right next to Ginny. He then sat down across from the couple. Jack was lighting up a cigarette, caught Eden's eye, and then put it down without lighting it. Ginny was pouring the champagne.

"Images are important to Jack, aren't they?" she asked Ruthie.

"Why sure. Aren't they important to everyone?"

"So then, being seen with someone as pretty as Ginny must be important to Jack too."

"Oh, I wouldn't worry about Ginny if I were you," Ruthie said nonchalantly. "I think I know Jack well enough to say he wouldn't take her back after she broke their engagement to go live abroad."

"They were engaged?" Eden felt an emptiness inside her chest. Why hadn't Jack told her he was once engaged? Was he trying to keep it a secret? Maybe Jack didn't mention it, because he was hoping Ginny would come back to him. And if he wanted her back, where did that leave her? After all, it was important for him to impress his father. He would do anything to impress the man. But would he go that far?

She overheard Jack telling his father he no longer wanted to get married. He seemed adamant about it. So, Jack wasn't the marrying kind? She put her hand on her belly, suddenly feeling alone and unwanted. She suddenly wondered if Jack really wanted her, other than for the obvious reasons. She felt out of place there, now. It was obvious his father didn't think much of foreigners and would never want her as a daughter-in-law. Now she started to wonder if Jack would ever want her for his wife.

"You're not worried, honey. About Ginny and Jack. Are you?" asked Ruthie.

"No. Why should I be?" She bit her lip and tried to fake a smile.

"Jack is a good guy," said Ruthie. "He's real. He doesn't like the fake kind of women like Ginny. He likes people who are real, like himself. Someone like you."

"Thanks, Ruthie," said Eden. "That's good to know."

"Sure, sweetie. Enjoy your birthday. I hear Jack's got some kind of big surprise to give you."

"Yeah," said Eden and laid a hand on her stomach. "So have I."

Ruthie left for the kitchen, and Eden stepped into Jack's empty office to try to regain her composure before she headed back out to the floor. Being pregnant was making her more emotional than she'd ever been before. Ruthie was right. Jack still wanted her. Didn't he?

She sat down on Jack's chair, and that was when she noticed the Bible. She picked it up and checked for the hidden contents. They were still there. It seemed Jack never discovered them. She doubted he'd ever even opened the book.

She needed a tissue but couldn't find one anywhere on Jack's messy desk. She opened the top drawer, hoping to find one. Instead, she found a slim white box with a bow on top. Scribbled on the box was her name, and the words Happy Birthday.

She looked to the door to see if anyone had noticed her coming into the office. It didn't seem so. She figured she'd just take a quick peek at Jack's present. She needed to see the big surprise he'd been wanting to give her. It would make her feel better about the whole situation with Ginny. It would give her the boost she needed to make it through the night. It would also give her the courage to tell Jack he was going to be a father.

The box was taped, and she used a fingernail to split the seal. She felt her heart beating in her throat, and she felt queasy in her stomach. But she had to know. She had to prove to herself that Jack cared for her. That he wanted her. That he wanted her enough to buy her a special present. She wanted to know she was the woman in his life.

She opened the box. Inside was an airline ticket with her name on it. It was for the end of next month. It was a ticket sending her home. Eden picked it up and looked under it, but there was nothing else. Just one ticket for her. One ticket for her to return to her homeland and leave Jack forever. He had intended to send her home before his father returned. He was embarrassed of her after all. He didn't want her there any more than he wanted to be known as a failure.

She was furious when Missy walked into the office.

"What's the matter, Eden? You look pretty upset."

"I am," she said, shoving the box into the drawer, not bothering to put it back together. "Jack's big surprise for my birthday is a ticket out of here."

"What?" said Missy. "Are you sure? That just doesn't sound like Jack."

"Check the drawer if you don't believe me. The ticket is all the proof I need. He was planning on sending me home before his father returned," she said. "But his father returned early. That must be why Jack looked so upset. He'd never meant for his father to meet me."

"Oh, Eden. I'm so sorry." Missy walked over and hugged her. "What are you going to do?"

Eden knew exactly what she had to do. Get out of there and get away from Jack before she made a fool of herself begging him to let her stay. He wanted her to go back, so she would. But she would leave by her own free will, not because he decided to send her.

Eden picked up the Bible sitting in front of her on the desk. She pulled the ticket out of the lining, leaving the letter and the book open and in plain sight.

"I'm going home to my family," she said. "I have a ticket my father bought me before he died. It's dated for tonight. It's an eight o'clock flight. If I leave now I should be able to make it."

"Eden, is this what you really want?"

Eden looked over to where Jack sat chatting with his father, sipping champagne with Ginny hanging on his arm. This wasn't the life for her. She would never get used to living here. She wanted to raise her child in her homeland. She wanted her baby to grow up knowing her customs and culture. Not an environment like this. She knew now it would be better to just go home and never even tell Jack about his child.

"Missy, can you give me a ride to the airport?"

"Well, sure, I guess. But don't you think you should talk to Jack first?"

"No. And don't you breathe a word of it to him either. I don't want him knowing anything about this until I'm up in the air and on my way home."

Eden got to her feet and hurried to the door. "I'm going to pack my things. Meet me out back with the car in five minutes."

Jack was having the worst time of his life. His father wasn't giving him a chance to talk. All he wanted to do was take his father aside and tell him about Eden. But the place was bustling with people, and his father insisted on greeting them all. And Ginny kept hanging on his arm, never leaving him for a moment.

He had seen the look on Eden's face when his father snubbed her. And he'd seen the way she'd put her head down and held her stomach like she was going to be sick when she found out about Ginny. He looked around the room but couldn't see Eden in the crowd. He had to get her on the side and talk to her before she took this whole thing the wrong way.

He should have told her about Ginny long ago, but he didn't expect to see his ex-fiancée again, so he didn't think it mattered. But he wanted to tell Eden now. He wanted to tell her every detail about every waking moment of his life. He wanted to tell her he loved her—something he had never said, but knew in his heart for a while now. It was her birthday, and he wanted to spend time with her and her alone. But his father came home a month early, and in ten minutes had already planned Jack's future.

"I'll talk to you later," Jack said, detaching Ginny from his arm and trying to get away from his father, talking to a crowd of people standing next to their table.

Alastair reached across the booth and pulled Jack down again. He poured him another glass of champagne. "Come now, Jack. I've been gone for a year. Don't tell me you're going to desert your old man already. Now tell me how you got this idea to make the place Peruvian. I absolutely love it. And I'm sure the crowd would like to hear the story too."

Jack felt a loyalty to his father and didn't want to disappoint him by not answering his questions. Not to mention the crowd of people by the table were egging him on. He started to tell them about Eden, when he saw her coming down the stairs in her old orange skirt, red jacket, manta on her back, sandals on her feet and that damned tall white hat on her head.

"Is that her?" asked Ginny, laughing at Eden. "She looks so pathetic in that get-up. It looks so worn and dirty. And that silly hat!"

"Enough!" said Jack as the crowd laughed along with Ginny. Eden glanced at him and he thought he saw tears in her eyes. He wanted to set the crowd straight, but something told him he needed to go to Eden instead.

"Eden!" Jack called, but she rushed out through the kitchen.

"Something's not right," Jack mumbled. "I've got to see what's going on."

Against his father's protests, Jack got up from the booth and made his way across the crowded room. Every time he took a step, someone stopped him to congratulate him on being the owner of the restaurant. He just excused himself and tried to get away. He burst into the kitchen. No Eden.

Alfredo looked at him from the stoves. "Looking for something, Señor Jack?"

"Did you see Eden come through here?"

"She rushed out of here into the back yard a minute ago. I called to her, but she just ignored me. She looked pretty upset."

"Damn!" He shouldn't have left her to go talk with his father. He should have just made his father wait. And what the hell was his father doing coming home early and unannounced, anyway? Jack hadn't had time to prepare for this situation. He had hoped that when the time came to introduce Eden to his father, he could introduce her as his fiancée.

He ran out the back door and caught a glimpse of Missy's car—the car that was once his, as it sped down the alley with Missy and Eden in it. He called after them, but they didn't seem to hear.

He stood there for a moment and listened to the night. He tuned out the sound of the city, squealing tires, beeping horns and all-around noise. Instead, he heard nothing but the sound of the crickets as they chirped. The moon was full, and the garden was in bloom. He could smell the sweet fragrance of the roses on the trellis over his head. The whole garden screamed of Eden. The once pitiful patch of dying grass now rose to the sky in glory because of Eden. It was an Incan empire calling out to him, telling him its hidden treasure had just driven out of his life.

Gaspar the cat slinked out of the shadows and rubbed its body against Jack's legs, purring softly.

"What do you want?" grumbled Jack. "If you're looking for food, I don't have any."

He could hear the sounds of the fiesta in the background, the laughing voices, the clatter of dishes, the Peruvian panpipe music. He felt so empty. So alone. He felt in his heart he'd done something terribly wrong, but he didn't know what. Eden had left without telling him where she was going. She had left in her native clothes and with her filled manta on her back. There was only one place she could be going and the thought horrified him.

He tore through the back door, raced through the kitchen, almost knocking Tisha down in the process. The sleeping baby wrapped in the manta on her back woke up and started crying. Her kids got under his feet, and he jumped over them as he made his way through the crowd and into his office.

Sure enough, the Bible lay open on his desk. He searched for the ticket in the lining. It was gone.

"Damn!" He pounded his fist against the desk, sinking into his chair, and cursing himself for not taking Eden to the table with his father and Ginny in the first place.

His father stepped into the office with a look of concern upon his brow.

"Jack. Is everything all right? I've never seen you so upset."

"It's Eden," he said. "She's gone. Without even a good-bye."

"Eden?" Alastair took a seat across from his son. "The hired help? That girl you introduced me to?"

"She wasn't the hired help. She was my girlfriend. More than my girlfriend. I was going to ask her tonight at the party to be my wife."

"Why didn't you tell me, son?"

"I was trying to. I didn't have a chance with the way you waltzed in here causing a scene and announcing to everyone I was going to marry Ginny."

Jack rose before his father could respond. "I need a car, Dad. Can I use your rental?"

"I took a limo from the airport."

"Shit!"

"Where's the Mercedes, son?"

"There's a lot to fill you in on," said Jack, "but before I do all that, I need to find some wheels."

He brushed past Ginny as he bolted out of the office.

"What's wrong, Jacky?" she cooed.

"Good-bye, Ginny," he ground out, making his way on to the floor, flagging down Ruthie.

"What's the matter?" Ruthie asked.

"I need to borrow your car," he told her.

"Sure," she said, "but I think its wedged in. The lot's double parked with the crowd we've got tonight."

"Forget it," he said, hurrying over to the bar where Nathan was mixing drinks. "I need the keys to your Harley," he told him. "Fast."

"Like hell," answered Nathan, putting the garnish on the drink and handing it to the waitress. "What's up?"

"It's Eden. She's gone to the airport and I've got to stop her before she gets on that plane."

"Let's go," said Nathan, throwing down the bar rag and heading for the back exit. "I'll give you a lift."

Chapter 23

Jack ran up to the gate with Nathan on his heels. "There's Missy," he said, making his way through the crowd like a quarterback dodging across a football field.

"Missy! Missy!" Jack called, but she kept staring out the terminal window. When he came to a halt next to her, he realized that she was watching a plane just taking off.

"No!" shouted Jack and grabbed Missy by the shoulders. "Don't tell me that was Eden's plane?"

"She's gone," said Missy.

Jack closed his eyes and leaned against the window. He'd failed again. He was too late, and now Eden was gone from his life forever. He turned to watch the plane lift off. With it went his hopes and dreams for the future.

"C'mon, Jack." Nathan laid a hand on Jack's shoulder. "Let's go home."

"I've got to catch another flight and meet up with her," said Jack. "This plane is probably going to have a lay-over in Florida. Maybe I can meet up with her there. I've got to find out."

He ran to talk to the woman behind the desk. But when the woman punched the information into the computer and shook her head, he knew it was over.

"I'm sorry, sir," she said, "but the plane isn't stopping until it gets to Jamaica. It's only stopping for a short time to load passengers before it goes on to Lima."

"Then get me a flight to Jamaica, fast. I've got to try to catch her."

The woman shook her head. "The next flight to Jamaica isn't until late tomorrow night, and it's already full."

"There's got to be some way for me to catch her," Jack told the woman. "Anything. Can't you find some flight that—"

The woman shook her head. "I'm sorry. I'm not going to be able to help you."

Jack never felt so miserable in his life. He saw the lights from the plane out the window as it disappeared into the dark sky. Eden was gone. Without even a good-bye. And there was nothing he could do about it.

"C'mon," said Nathan, hand on Jack's shoulder. "I'll take you home."

❧

Jack sat alone with his feet on his desk, finishing off the last of the bottle of bourbon, trying to drown his sorrows. He'd given the apartment to his father to stay in while he was here. He couldn't bear to lie in the bed again if Eden wasn't by his side. Ginny had taken the hint and left the restaurant before he returned from the airport. The restaurant was closed now and all was quiet. The grand opening had been a huge success, which should have made Jack happy, but right now he didn't give a damn.

"Good-night, Jack." Ruthie popped her head in the office on her way out. "Everyone's gone. You want me to lock up the back door on my way out?"

"No. I'll get it, Ruthie." Jack downed the contents of his glass and tried to squeeze a last drop out of the bottle.

Ruthie came in and laid a hand on Jack's shoulder. "I'm sorry to hear Eden left you," she said. "This place won't be the same without her."

"Yeah." Jack stared at the glass and ran his finger around the rim. "Nothing's for sure, Ruthie. That's why you've got to just live each day to the fullest."

"That's what Eden always used to say," Ruthie agreed. "Hey, did you know Tisha's husband showed up here tonight?"

"What'd the bum want? To drive the knife deeper into the poor girl's heart? I didn't figure he'd ever come back after he left her and the kids for the bottle."

Jack noticed Ruthie staring at his own empty bottle.

"Just the opposite, Jack. He wants her back. A second chance. The kids were so happy to see him."

"That's wonderful." Jack really couldn't care less at the moment.

"He's staying at Tisha's place above the garage tonight. He's going to go out in the morning and look for a job. Seems he wants to start his life over."

"Don't we all," mumbled Jack.

"I was wondering, Jack—"

"Have him start tomorrow. We could use another bartender. And since I hear the guy was a drunk he ought to know how to make the damned drinks."

"Thanks, Jack. And would you mind if he—"

"He can stay with Tisha and the kids above the garage. But once they're back on their feet I'm going to have to start charging rent."

"I'll tell them on the way out."

"You do that." Jack brought the bottle to his lips, realized it was empty and tossed it into the trash.

"You know, Jack. That's not going to bring her back to you."

"She doesn't want to come back," he said. "Why would she want a failure like me? If she did, she wouldn't have left in the first place."

"You're not a failure," Ruthie assured him. "Just look what you've done to this place. Your father was so impressed he gave you the restaurant."

"She made the restaurant a success, not me. If she hadn't come along I would have run it into the ground. I don't belong here, Ruthie, and you know it."

"What! What are you saying? I don't like to hear you talking this way. You just stop feeling sorry for yourself right now, Jack Talon. That kind of attitude never helped anyone."

"You're probably right," agreed Jack. "You're always right, Ruthie. And I'm just lucky I've had you to talk to about all my problems."

She squeezed his shoulder gently. "You know you can always come to me with your troubles."

"I love her," he blurted out. "And without her I'm not even sure I have the will to go on."

Jack rubbed his face tiredly, then reached in his pocket and pulled out a golden wedding band, holding it up for Ruthie to see.

"This was for Eden?" she asked, taking it in her hand and examining it.

"It was the damned big surprise I was going to give her for her birthday. That and this." He pulled open the desk drawer to get the ticket and realized the box was lying open inside.

Ruthie put the ring on the desk and looked at the ticket over Jack's shoulder.

"I don't understand, Jack. You were going to propose to her and then send her home?"

"I had another ticket coming, Ruthie. One for me." Jack stared at the ticket in the open box. There was only one person who would open a present that was addressed to Eden.

"Shit!" He slammed the drawer shut, and Ruthie looked at him oddly.

"She must have found the ticket and believed I was sending her home—by herself. She couldn't have known I had another ticket for me coming in the mail."

"Jack, you need to go after her."

"I already tried that earlier. But now I'm not so sure. What if I get there and she doesn't want me, Ruthie?"

"Do you love her?"

"I told you I did!"

"Then that's just the chance you're going to have to take. If you don't go after her, you'll never know if she loves you. And I'd hate to see you living in misery for the rest of your life for not even trying."

Jack barely heard Ruthie saying good-bye as she walked out the door.

He picked up the ring, studying it. It was a plain ring, but it was all he could afford right now. Would Eden want it? Would she want to be his wife and move away from the mountains of Cuzco to come live by his side and help him run his restaurant? He wondered. She said the Quechua's didn't have much but they were happy. Jack had just about everything now—except Eden—and he was miserable.

He didn't know how long he sat there staring at the ring, before he got up, put the ring in his pocket and headed out into Eden's garden.

He sat down in the middle of a patch of flowers and breathed in their scent. Her scent. She was the land and everything that grew on it. She was the sunshine in his life.

"Jack? Is that you?"

He saw Tisha coming down the stairs from the garage apartment. She was in her housecoat and bare feet. She had the sleeping baby in her arms.

"Yeah, it's me."

"I just wanted to thank you for giving my husband a job. Ruthie told me all about it. And thank you once again for letting us stay here."

"Yeah, sure."

She turned to go, then stopped. He could see the whites of her eyes in the moonlight against her dark skin.

"I have something to tell you, Jack. Something I think you should know. I promised Eden I wouldn't say anything, but I just have to."

Jack looked up wondering what the hell she was talking about. She almost sounded as if Eden told her some sort of secret.

"Tell me, Tisha. If it has to do with Eden, I have to know."

"She's pregnant, Jack. With your baby."

He jumped to his feet and grabbed Tisha by the shoulders. The motion woke her baby—Baby Eden, and it started to cry.

"Are you sure, Tisha? I've got to know for sure."

"Positive," she said, trying to hush the baby. "She was so excited, she was going to tell you tonight when she got you alone."

"Oh, no!" Jack felt sick. "That was the surprise she was talking about. And she thought my surprise was sending her home. She had no idea I was going to ask her to marry me."

"I'm sorry," said Tisha and started to head back to her place.

"Wait!" Jack called. "Tisha, did she seem happy she was pregnant?"

"She was ecstatic," Tisha said, bouncing her crying baby. "She just wasn't sure you'd be, Jack. She was a little nervous to tell you. She said she had nothing to offer."

"Nothing to offer? Didn't she realize she's the best thing that ever happened to me?"

"I guess not, Jack." The baby cried louder, and Tisha excused herself. "I hope everything works out for you," she said as she left.

Jack felt his blood pumping through him in a newfound energy. He was going to be a father! He and Eden were going to be parents.

He sat down in the flower patch again and lay back to think things over. He was surprised to see so many tiny stars winking at him from the city-lit sky. Such a vast sky. Such a huge world. And he was just a speck on the surface. He wondered if Eden was looking at those same stars right now. The stars that spanned the universe and beyond. And he wondered why, in all his years, he had never even noticed them before now.

He was suddenly seeing things he never had before. Eden was right when she told him money wouldn't bring him happiness. He had everything he ever wished for and he was still miserable. Without Eden, he'd always be miserable.

He jumped to his feet and took one last look at Eden's garden. His love for her had grown just like the seeds she'd planted. He would go to her, find her, if it took him the rest of his life to track her down. He would tell her he loved her

Chapter 24

It had been weeks now since Eden left Chicago, and with each and every passing day she was more convinced she'd done the wrong thing. She took one last look at Jack's photo in her locket and clicked it shut. She missed him so much it hurt. But still, it felt good to be back in the mountains of Peru.

She worked the fields next to her mother and the other women of the village and watched her brother Cirilo and her sister Isidora chasing each other, rousing up the alpacas. The alpacas looked at them through their curious eyes and darted out of the way in an attempt to escape the confusion.

Eden laughed and realized it felt good to be back with her family. She carried little Pia on her back in her manta. Her baby sister was getting older now and she wouldn't carry her much longer. Soon Pia would be running around and playing with Eden's own child. She put her hand on her stomach and felt the baby kick. A wave of excitement washed through her. If only Jack could be here to feel the kick as well.

She'd told her mother about Jack. She'd also told her about the baby. Her mother understood, having gone through the same thing with an American man so long ago. But her mother told her it was the way it had to be. She never could have married Jonathan Starke, because the Quechuas only married among themselves. It took ten years for any of the native men to ask for her mother's hand, and Eden knew it was because she had a daughter of mixed blood.

She wondered if her baby would be an outcast. She put her hand on her stomach, sad that the child would never get to know its father. Eden would never have enough money to buy a ticket back to the States. She had made her decision to leave and now she would never see Jack again. But it was what he wanted, she reminded herself.

Her mother called to her from the house, and Eden made her way across the field. Pabla Ramirez took Pia from Eden's manta and told her that her uncle had found an American wandering around at the train stop. Since none of them knew the English language, they didn't know what he was saying. But her uncle recognized the name the man kept repeating. Eden. And so he had shown the man the way to their little village in the mountains.

Eden's heart skipped a beat as she listened to her mother's story. Could this be Jack? Would he be crazy enough to venture so far into a foreign land trying to find her in the mountains of Peru?

She heard the squeals of laughter from the village children, and saw them jumping around a man in a poncho as he blew up balloons and tossed them out to them. Then she saw that the man in the poncho wore a pair of mirrored sunglasses. A smile came to her face and tears to her eyes.

"Jack?" She hurried toward him.

He looked at her coming across the field and removed his sunglasses. She stopped in her tracks and they both stared at each other, his eyes interlocking with hers and reaching down to her very soul.

"Eden!" he called and waved an arm. He pushed through the horde of kids and ran toward her. The children thought he wanted to race and ran after him squealing with laughter.

He scooped her off her feet. Laughing, she held on to her hat as he twirled her around. When he finally set her down, he pulled her into his arms for a kiss. Her hat fell off in the process, but she did nothing to retrieve it.

By now the kids were crowding around them, and Eden couldn't hear a word Jack was trying to say. He took his sunglasses and showed them to the kids, then threw them as far as he could, and the kids rushed off to find them.

"That should keep them busy for a while." He laughed, but immediately was serious again, as he looked into her eyes.

"What are you doing here?" she asked. "I can't believe you found me."

"I would have searched to the ends of the earth to find you, Eden. I need to ask you something and I wanted to ask you face to face."

"You nut!" she said, hitting him on the arm playfully. "What did you need to know? How the scoring system works in sapo, or just the recipe for ceviche?"

"Neither." He dug his hand into the front pocket of his white jeans. "I already know both of those things, Eden. What I don't know is this."

He held up a gold band. A wedding ring if Eden wasn't mistaken. He then took her hands in his and got down on one knee.

"Will you marry me, Eden Ramirez? Will you be my wife and mother of my children?"

Eden wiped the tears from her eyes and pulled him to his feet. "Get up already, Jack. You're getting your white pants dirty."

"I don't give a damn about that. All I care about is you."

"But what about the ticket I found in your drawer? You were going to send me home."

"I had another ticket in the mail," he explained. "For me. I was coming with you, Eden. And I was also going to give you this ring the night of your birthday, but you ran off."

"You mean—you wanted to marry me then?" she asked.

"I love you, Eden. I wanted you then, and I want you now. Please say you'll marry me."

"I love you, too, Jack. But I'm not sure it'll work."

"Why not?" he asked. "If two people are in love, they can make anything work."

"But this is my homeland, Jack. I think I want to raise my children here—to learn my people's ways. To play in the mountains and open air. To feel the freedom I feel every time I look around me. I'm not sure I'm ready to come back to the States."

"You don't have to. I've already decided to stay here with you."

Eden couldn't believe what she was hearing. Jack living in the mountains of Peru? She laughed at the thought. "But what about your restaurant? And your father and friends back home?"

"What restaurant?" Jack asked, and Eden realized his father mustn't have given it to him after all.

"I'm sorry," she said.

"About what? My father's moved back to Greece, and hell if I'm going there. Too much of a culture shock, you know."

"Oh really?" She laughed, looking at her surroundings. Her mother and family stood by their simple, small house, and the men worked in the fields while the children took a break from work and played with Jack's sunglasses and the balloons. The mountains stretched out over the vast sky, bright green rolling meadows as far as the eye could see. Women sat at their looms weaving ponchos and the alpacas wandered around looking for food.

"Besides," said Jack. "I sold my restaurant to Missy and Nathan. They decided to form a partnership and are taking over the place. They said we can come visit whenever we want."

"That's great," she said, "I guess. Jack, do you realize what you're committing yourself to by marrying me and staying in Peru?"

"I don't care," he said. "As long as you're with me."

"The Quechua's don't accept outsiders to live in their village. We'd have to move to Cuzco or Arequipa or one of the larger towns."

"That would be perfect," he said. "Then we could start up our own restaurant here. And we'd still be close enough to your family for them to see our baby."

Eden suddenly realized what Jack had said. "You know I'm pregnant," she said. "Tisha told you, didn't she?"

"You know women can never keep their mouths shut," he said. "And by the way, I'm a little hurt you didn't tell me yourself."

"I planned on telling you, but I was afraid."

"Afraid? What on earth for?"

"Well, you always wanted to use protection when we made love. I figured you didn't want a baby."

"Then you don't know me very well, Eden. I want that baby, and you, more than anything in the world."

"You'd be giving up so much, though."

"I'd be gaining more than you'll ever know. You were the one who taught me money couldn't buy happiness. You taught me so much, Eden. But if you don't want me, I'll understand. Just say the word and I'll leave you forever and never bother you again."

"Ari," said Eden.

Jack looked at her and raised a brow.

"If you're going to be living here, you'd better start to learn Quechua," she said. "After all, my family doesn't speak any English."

"Then, ari means yes?" Jack asked carefully.

Eden smiled and answered, "sí."

"That one I know." He let out a loud whoop that caused everyone to come running. He took the ring and put it on Eden's finger, then pulled her in his arms and kissed her. It felt so right to Eden, so good to have Jack's arms around her once again. She knew with Jack, she was truly home.

Her eyes opened wide when she felt the baby kick. She took Jack's hand and laid it against her womb. "Feel the way your son kicks, Jack."

He kept his hand still for a moment and then asked, "How do you know it's a boy?"

"I don't," she answered. "But whatever it is, it'll be strong as an ox."

Her family joined them, and she introduced Jack to her mother and stepfather, to her siblings and the rest of the relatives. They looked at him cautiously as he waved and smiled, not understanding a word that was said. Then they returned to the fields to work.

"They'll get used to you eventually," Eden told him. "And by Quechua standards, we've already shown it'll be a fruitful marriage."

Jack got to his knees and kissed the baby in her womb. She liked the way it felt to have his hot breath so close to her thighs.

"Jack," she said, looking around. "We'd better find somewhere private to go if you're going to be doing that."

He stood up and pulled her against him. "What?" he asked. "All I was doing was kissing our baby."

"There'll be plenty of time for that later. Right now we have to find a place to live."

"Well, maybe you can show me around Cuzco. With luck, we'll be able to get a place where we can start up a little restaurant."

"I like that idea," said Eden. "Maybe near the train depot, where the tourists will stop on their way to Machu Picchu."

"And we'll serve American food," added Jack. "Just to be different."

Eden laughed again and found herself the happiest girl in the world. She was with the man she loved, and where once she was a foreigner in his land, now he was one in hers. This would be very interesting, but if anyone could pull it off, it was Jack. He'd probably be the most prosperous restaurant owner in the country. And she'd be right there by his side to help him.

"Now we need a name for our new restaurant," said Eden. "Got any suggestions?"

"I know exactly what to name it," he said in a low voice and kissed her on the forehead. "We're going to call it... Eden's Garden."

To My Readers

I hope you enjoyed Jack and Eden's story. *Eden's Garden* was inspired by a trip I took to Peru years ago with my husband.

Peru is magical, mystical, and the people and their culture captured my interest as well as my heart. That's why I knew I had to bring this part of my life to you through my writing.

Machu Picchu, the Lost City of the Incas, was like a dream. A place so high in the Andes that the double rainbow and clouds were below me. I was lucky enough to be able to have my own photography of this site used on the book's cover. The high mountain in the background is Huayna Picchu. We climbed that mountain and found ourselves sitting atop the world, literally. (And there really are flies up there.)

Nights at Machu Picchu are so gloriously dark that trillions of bright stars in the heavens are visible against the velvet sky.

The people of Cuzco are colorful and intriguing-their music lively, their lives simple, their food unique. I even roamed onto a back street where the local venders sell to their own people to find the colorful manta the model is wearing on the cover.

Thank you for sharing my memories of this wonderful journey through Eden's Garden. I hope Peru finds a special place in your heart as it did for me.

Elizabeth Rose

Order your favorite Genesis
Press titles directly from us!
Visit our web site for the latest
information
www.genesis-press.com
or call toll-free
1.888.463.4461

Broken
by Dar Tomlinson
ISBN 1-58571-002-4
$24.95 Hardcover
Winner of the Hemingway First Novel Award

Zac Abriendo had it all: A wife, a son, and a job he loved. His world was grounded in a deeply rooted commitment to work and family that spanned generations. His days were spent on the Gulf shrimping with his father. His nights were divided between computer classes at the local community college and his duties as a father and husband. All that changed the day Carron Fitzpatrick walked into his life.

Carron was everything that Zac wasn't. She was rich. She was Anglo. She was cold and calculating. And she would stop at nothing to get what she wanted. And she wanted Zac.

Critics have called Dar Tomlinson the "new voice" in women's fiction. With *Broken*, she gives readers a dark and disturbing look into basic drives and motives that affect us all, revealing a depth and introspection which goes far beyond her previously published novels.

Finding Isabella
by A.J. Garrotto
ISBN 1-58571-005-9
$8.95

Following the untimely deaths of her adoptive parents, Analisa Marconi begins her voyage of self-discovery by traveling to the island of Santo Sangre to find her birth mother. In the midst of that search she finds unexpected romance in the arms of opera singer, and local icon, Arturo Cristobal.

When the nature of her visit to the island is learned, Analisa is kidnapped by a militant anti-adoption organization called *Los Dejados* ("Those Left Behind") and given a "life sentence" of forced child-bearing. Can she escape and find her way back to Arturo and the life she left behind?

Set in Southern California, the Caribbean, and Spain's Costa del Sol, *Finding Isabella* is the inspiring story of a young woman's quest for life, love, and her own true identity.